D1097397

"Harvey, is that you?"

She spoke into the darkness, the words catching in her throat. A sudden soft noise shattered the stillness. Someone had to be there.

Harvey, she thought again, her heart pounding, not daring to speak. But how could it be? He was miles away, trying to avoid being picked up by the police on some silly charge.

Wasn't he?

Her heart jumped with terror. The snow crackled under heavy steps. Someone was coming up the path . . .

Not Me, Inspector

HELEN REILLY

MB
A MACFADDEN-BARTELL BOOK

A Macfadden Book............1971

THIS IS THE COMPLETE TEXT
OF THE ORIGINAL EDITION.

Macfadden-Bartell Corporation
A subsidiary of Bartell Media Corporation
205 East 42nd Street, New York, New York, 10017

©, Copyright, 1959, by Helen Reilly.
All rights reserved. Published by
arrangement with Random House, Inc.
Printed in the U.S.A.

Library of Congress Catalog Card Number: 59-10802

Not Me, Inspector

ONE

On the day it happened there were plenty of warnings but they were all masked. There was the snow, for instance. The snow meant nothing to Harvey Allert and his wife Mercedes, except perhaps, in a city like New York, the nuisance of sloppy pavements and the difficulty of getting cabs.

The Allerts were often described by their wide circle of friends as the perfect couple living a perfect life in a perfect little house, a jewel of a house in a court on Murray Hill. They were fun people, everybody who was anybody knew them and they knew everybody worth knowing. They were both young and attractive and gay. Dace Allert, slim and dark and graceful, was in her late twenties, and Harvey, a big, handsome, open-handed fellow, was in his middle thirties. There was no trouble about money, they were rolling—people said Harvey's father had left him the earth when he died.

If this picture was slightly rose-colored there was at least some truth in it. Harvey's father hadn't left them the earth when he was gathered to his forefathers several years earlier. He had left his only son fifty thousand dollars outright and an income of twelve thousand a year. The bulk of his estate had gone to his second wife,

Elfrida, for her life, after which it would revert to Harvey. But as the second Mrs. Allert was frail—she had been a semi-invalid for years—it didn't look as though Harvey would have to wait too long for the big money. And then a surprising development took place.

Harvey Allert Senior had been a strong-minded, strong-willed man and what he said went. Shortly after his remarriage he decided that his second wife was delicate, that exertion or strain of any kind was bad for her and that her proper environment was under glass. He was the director and handed out the parts and she was devoted to him, so that had been her role. Actually there was nothing wrong with her but a very slight heart condition, an ethereal look and a tendency to anemia. New doctors, new treatments and a new life—after her husband's death Elfrida became a new woman and blossomed like a rose.

This put the younger Allerts' noses rather out of joint financially, but Harvey took it in his stride. He and his stepmother were good friends and had always got along well and whatever his other faults he thought very little about money per se. People who have been used to it often don't. It is there when you need it, a wall at your back; that is what matters.

Suddenly the wall was no longer there. Elfrida Allert had never had to handle finances. That had been done by her husband. She learned very quickly. She had only a life interest in the estate, she couldn't touch the principal, but she could do what she liked with the more than substantial income. One of the first things she did after she took over the helm was to charge Harvey rent for the house in the court on Murray Hill.

Harvey had assumed that the house was his, that it had been a wedding present from his father on his marriage to Dace; it was too small for the older Allerts at that time of their lives and neither of them cared to live in New York. If this was so, the late Harvey père had failed to put anything in writing and as things stood the Murray Hill house belonged to the estate, which was in Elfrida's hands. To have to stump up four hundred a month on top of their other expenses was a blow—at any rate to Dace Allert, who was beginning to worry seriously about finances.

The fifty thousand in cash that Harvey had inherited outright from his father had vanished like smoke, the twelve thousand a year from the trust fund his father had set up melted like snow—and Harvey's own intake was, not to put too fine a point on it, fitful. He never stayed very long in a job; he couldn't seem to find anything that really suited him. Dace didn't know Harvey's stepmother well but what she had seen of the older woman she had liked. Elfrida Allert didn't seem to be either greedy or grasping and her sudden demand that they pay rent for the house struck Dace as odd and out of character.

She said, "I can't imagine what kind of woman your stepmother *is*, Harvey. She can't possibly need the money, and we most emphatically do. I have half a notion to write and tell her what I think of it."

Harvey had been much more furious than she was in the beginning but his first sense of violent outrage had passed. He grinned and threw up his hands. "For heaven's sakes, don't do anything, Dace. It will only get Elfrida's back up. Actually she's not a bad old duck, it's just that she's so terribly in earnest about everything—and anyhow it's only a phase. She's drunk with power. She'll get over it."

Dace had wanted to give up the house, pointing out that an apartment would be cheaper—they could get rid of the maids, for instance, and there would be no fuel bills—but Harvey wouldn't hear of it. His father and his own mother had lived in the little house during their few years together and he had been born there. He said no, said, "We'll have to retrench, for a while, until the old girl comes round—or conks out. Now let's see what a little of the old brain power will do." He got a pad and pencil and went to work.

The plan he drew up looked wonderful on paper, and Harvey was enthusiastic about it. Dace was cynical. But very much to her surprise Harvey did try to seriously reduce his spending. He eliminated his expensive downtown lunches and had the cook make him sandwiches, which he solemnly took to the office. He stopped playing cards at the club, he rescinded a large order he had sent his tailor and he crossed off the new car he had been contemplating. And with it all—and he was not a patient

9

man and hated what he called penny-pinching—a subject on which he and Dace had had more than one quarrel—he remained cheerful and in a good humor with the glass set at fair. "You'll see, Dace," he assured her, "we'll manage."

But they didn't manage. Their basic expenditure was too high and had gone on too long. They couldn't stop entertaining altogether or, for instance, cut off such things as contributions that were expected of them—things like that. Also bills Harvey hadn't calculated on kept coming in, and with the added burden of the four-hundred-dollar monthly rent they went steadily deeper into the red.

And then, in January, Elfrida had her accident.

The day was January the eighth.

Elfrida was in New York briefly. She had flown in from Arizona and was on her way to the Allert farm in Duchess County where she intended to remain through the spring. She was staying at the Plaza. She phoned Harvey at his office on the morning of the seventh and he went to see her there.

When Dace got home at five o'clock that afternoon from a boring bridge lunch for some charity whose name she didn't know or had forgotten, there was a car in front of the house on the court. The hood was up and in the fading light Harvey was bending over the engine. He heard her coming and stood erect, wiping a smudge of grease from his chin. His bright brown hair was rumpled and there was color in his face. How like a handsome boy he was, she thought with a pang—a boy, just that.

The car was new, a little foreign affair, very smart. Looking at it Dace's heart sank. "Oh, Harvey, you didn't . . ."

He laughed. "Don't be foolish. Of course not. It's a custom-built Torshe-Hamton. Elfrida bought it last summer—it was in storage and I got it out for her. Isn't she a beauty, isn't she? Look at those lines, and has she got power."

He said Elfrida was driving up to the farm the next day and wanted him to check the Torshe for her. Harvey was crazy about cars and he was an expert with them, far better than most mechanics. He said all the Torshe needed was a little tightening up here and there, and returned to his tinkering lovingly. Later on he reported back to Elfrida, put the car in a garage and on the following morning, the morning of the eighth, he drove it to the Plaza and left it with the doorman before going on downtown to his office.

At a little before ten it started to snow, lightly at first, and it didn't look as though it would amount to much, but at around noon the wind shifted and by two o'clock the storm had begun in earnest.

Harvey got home early that day and the moment he entered the house Dace was afraid there was going to be trouble. She was in the living room finishing a book she wanted to return to the lending library—she rented books now instead of buying them—when Harvey walked in whistling. This outward display of well-being, contentment, was a sure sign that he was up to something, or going to spring something that he didn't think she'd like. He was in high, almost boisterous spirits and his greeting was exuberant.

"Here you are . . . Good. I was afraid you'd be out gallivanting."

He kissed her, lit a cigarette, went over to the mantel and looked at his reflection in the mirror, or at hers, Dace couldn't tell which. He said with elaborate carelessness that there was not much doing at the office when he went back after lunch and there didn't seem to be any sense hanging around, and wandered over to the window. The snow was coming down hard, a slanting white curtain you couldn't see through. The brick wall hemming in the court, the leafless trees beyond it, were invisible. There was nothing but the snow. It seemed to please, excite Harvey.

"Nice, isn't it?" He gestured at the whirling flakes driving down. "Reminds me of when I was a kid and I couldn't wait to get out in it . . . Dace, pay attention—put down that book and listen to me. You know what I was thinking on the way uptown."

She said, "No, what?" and he said, "How would you like to take a trip somewhere south, St. Augustine, or the Keys, or maybe the Gulf Coast?"

So this was what Harvey had been leading up to; Dace sighed inwardly. Whenever he got bored or tired of

11

keeping his nose to the grindstone he proposed a trip somewhere. In their present financial state such a thing was about as practical as asking whether she'd like a trip to Venus. He was waiting eagerly for her answer. . . . Temporize, handle him gently.

She said, "Later on if we can manage it, it would be nice . . ."

He smoothed his hair with an impatient hand. "I don't mean later on, I mean right now. The Benz is sitting around there in the garage and the snow isn't deep yet. We could throw some things into a couple of bags and be off in half an hour. It would do us both a world of good, we're in too much of a rut, we haven't had any fun in a long while. Think how swell it will be to get into the sun. . . . How about it? What do you say?"

Dace put her book aside, settled back in her chair and looked at him. She said mildly, "In the first place, Harvey, we happen to have people coming for dinner tonight, Olivia and Gerald, you asked them yourself." Olivia was her own cousin and Harvey liked her, and Gerald Straws was one of his oldest and closet friends.

"Call them," Harvey said promptly. "Put them off. They won't care. Tell them we're dead, or gone to Alaska . . . Or I'll call them. Right now. O.K.?"

His face was alight, his blue eyes bright and eager. The prospect of change, any kind of change, sent his spirits soaring. He had been awfully good about economizing and for him, patient, but what he proposed was out of the question. Dace reached for a cigarette. Careful, she thought, don't provoke an explosion. She smiled at him lazily.

"I don't want to ask impertinent questions, my pet, but what are we—what would we use for money?"

Harvey laughed. "Ha, got you." He was triumphant. He put his hand in his breast pocket, drew out his wallet and spread it. Dace looked at it in astonishment. It was crammed to overflowing with cash—and yesterday morning she had had to give him a ten out of the housekeeping money to get downtown with, and there would be nothing coming in for two weeks.

"Corn in Egypt," he said, patting the wallet fondly.

"Where did you get it?" she asked wonderingly. "How much is there?"

"One thousand bucks, simoleons, coin of the realm. Step up, ladies and gents, and see the lucky winner. My mudder came in at the track and brought home the bacon, a long shot, on the nose. It was pouring down there. Pleased with your husband, girl, what? Now do you know why I thought we'd celebrate, strike while the iron is hot, and take a run south? It's going to be good to get out of the city, and if we step on it we can be well on our way before dark. I'll go and call your cousin and Gerald."

Dace looked past him at a dazzle of flakes between the long, green satin curtains with a feeling of something like despair. Just when you thought Harvey was changing his ways, that he was sitting down and facing things, you were fooled again. This time she had been almost confident. They were in debt up to their eyeballs. A thousand dollars wouldn't go far but it would settle a few of the more pressing bills, the grocer and the milk and the tailor—she had taken to crossing the street so as not to have to go past his shop. Try and get Harvey to hear reason, give her the money. "Harvey, listen to me for a moment. . . ."

That was as far as she got. At her first word Harvey blew up, going into one of his rages with the facility and swiftness of long habit. He had almost reached the door. He turned and came back. The symptoms were all there. His face had gone white and his eyes were lightless bits of stone. Crossing to the hearth he stood there rigid, looking at her, his shoulders hunched, his hands deep in his pockets. A vein in one temple pulsed in and out. And then it began. The accusations, epithets, poured out in a steady stream. She was a this and that, she had married him for his money and when she found he didn't have as much as she thought he had, she had turned sour, had turned into a penny-pinching shrew. She had nothing of her own, not a damned cent, he paid the bills and he was the boss and he was damn well going to stay that way and she might as well know it now as any other time. And while they were on the subject, there was another thing he wanted her to know. He wasn't blind. Men—there was always a man—even his own friends weren't exempt. Gerald Straws

13

was coming to dinner, was he? That was why she didn't want to go anywhere. She couldn't pull the wool over his eyes, she needn't think he hadn't noticed her the other night with Gerald, the way she kept looking at him, the way they had danced was enough to make a dog sick . . . It was disgusting, it . . .

As his rage mounted his accusations became more definite. Violence would come next. It did.

"Answer me," he shouted.

Dace simply sat and looked at him. Whatever she did would be the wrong thing. . . . When he was in one of these moods nothing could stop him, nothing. This time it was worse than usual. She had never seen him quite so bad. . . . No doubt the maids were listening. . . . They wouldn't have to try very hard.

He shouted at her again. He was shaking. He brought a fist down on the mantel shelf. The blue ginger jar teetered. He snatched the jar up and hurled it to the floor. As it struck the hearth and crashed, the front doorbell rang.

It stopped Harvey in mid flight. He broke off, stared at her redly for a moment, then slammed out of the room and up the stairs.

The servants *had* heard. As Dace went to answer the bell, one of them—it was Gertrude—appeared in the gloom at the rear of the hall. She looked scared. Dace said, "I'll take it, Gertrude," and went to the door. It was only the mailman. The mail consisted of a sheaf of bills. Dace put them on the table under the mirror and glanced at her watch. She had a sudden longing to get away from Harvey and turmoil, get out into the air and feel the wind on her face. It was only ten minutes of four, and Olivia and Gerald Straws wouldn't be along until cocktail time. A pity anyone was coming, with Harvey in one of his takings, but he was fond of Olivia and wouldn't want to appear in a bad light in front of her—and without her there as a whipping post in the meantime, his fury would die down. She opened the closet door. Boots, a scarf, a heavy coat; two minutes later she was out in the street.

Snow was still falling blindingly and it was bitter cold. Dace struck west aimlessly and then south, with no definite goal except to stay out of the house and away from Harvey until he got hold of himself and came to.

These rages of his had to run their course. Short or long, the result would be the same in the end. His fury would be followed later by remorse, self-accusation, penitence, a plea for forgiveness and a promise that it would never happen again. "You're an angel, Dace, I don't know how you put up with me. I'm a brute, a beast. But don't ever leave me, swear you won't."

She had no intention of leaving Harvey. If almost three years ago she had married without sufficient reflection, because her father had just died—and because of that other thing—and she was alone and life seemed to have lost its meaning, the fault was hers, not his. She wasn't in love with him but she was fond of him and she had gone into it with her eyes open. So she had expected Harvey to develop, to change and grow, had she? Lots of people expected lots of things and didn't get them. So you made do with what you had . . . Affection and pity—pity for the capabilities in Harvey that had withered on the vine—weren't too bad. In his good moods Harvey was a pleasant companion, amiable and sunny and sometimes very sweet. Why make a song and dance of these occasional blowups of his? Today's was the first in quite a while, it was also the worst.

Snow blew in her face and she pulled her fur scarf up around her ears and buried her chin in it. Shortly after their marriage she had spoken to their doctor, Herb Grant, about Harvey's blowups, but Grant was a conservative anyhow and he'd known Harvey for a long while. He said, "He had too much too young, he didn't have to face up to things, and it held him back. There's a lot of the boy in him still, but he'll steady down." Today's outburst *was* the first in two or three months. Her refusal to fall in with his idea of dashing south had triggered it; she wondered whether there was something else, whether something had happened at the office . . . Perhaps he had thrown up his job.

Deeply engrossed in her own thoughts and oblivious of her surroundings Dace woke suddenly to the fact that it was now completely dark and that she had been walking for a long while. Her legs were tired and she was chilled to the bone, her hands and feet were blocks of ice. If anything, the snow was coming down harder than when she

15

had started out. The street lamps were on but they were mere glimmers wreathed in white. Where was she?

An illuminated clock swimming into view said five-ten. The clock told her that she was at the corner of Madison and Thirty-third. Only a few more blocks to go; she had turned north without being aware of it.

It was Thursday and the maids would have gone by now but if Olivia and Gerald Straws had already arrived Harvey would let them in. She thought of his accusation about Gerald and herself and half smiled. Gerald was Harvey's friend, not hers, and it was for Harvey he came to the house. Not that she didn't like Gerald Straws. She did. What was more important was that he was a steadying influence on Harvey; he could get him back on the track with a few quiet, downright words when she was helpless. And that was all there was to it, and Harvey knew it, but when he was in a bad mood he would say anything, no matter how far-fetched.

Out in front the colored lights of the Rockingham bar winked on and off faintly, like Christmas bulbs in a dream. As she turned the corner and advanced toward the court a man standing near the gates moved in her direction. He was a vague bulk without feature in the drive of the snow. She was veering to pass him when he spoke.

"Dace."

At the sound of his voice an electric shock went through her. The man was Hugh Clavering.

TWO

The last time Dace had seen Hugh Clavering she had asked him not to come to the house, or to any other place where they were likely to meet, and he had concurred. That was almost two years ago. It no longer mattered. It was in another dimension, had taken on the outlines of a blurred but remembered dream. What there had been between them was dead, done for, over, finished. Other affairs, other interests had filled its place.

"Why, Hugh," she exclaimed when she got her breath. "I didn't know you were in New York. When last I heard, you were in Arizona or somewhere—I think it was Olivia who told me." It was at Olivia's that she and Hugh had first met. Dace smiled up at him through the snow.

Hugh stood looking down at her, snow dusting the shoulders of his coat. His face was in shadow. He was scrutinizing her, almost as though he had never seen her before, and there was an odd intentness in his gaze.

"That job ended. I've been back for quite a while. . . . Dace—I've got to talk to you."

His voice was clipped, abrupt; he was under strain of some sort. Dace was disconcerted and uneasy. Surely Hugh didn't think she was going to start that all over again—but no, certainly not. Not only did he understand women too well but he was too intuitive and too clever for that.

She said lightly, "Talk to me—of course, come on into the house, it's only a step."

Hugh shook his head. "I've just come from there. I saw your cousin Olivia. She said you were out but she expected you any moment, and I've been waiting here on the chance that you might come along."

"Oh Hugh, I can't. I'm late now. . . ."

He rode her down in the same old way. "It's important, Dace."

She wasn't having any. "Sorry, Hugh, but I've really got to . . ."

Again he wouldn't let her finish. "It's about Elfrida, Dace."

She had started to move. She came to a halt. Hugh had been married to Elfrida's niece, Dolly, who was now dead. It was a tragedy. Dolly had died of leukemia at the age of twenty-nine. Dace said wonderingly, "Elfrida?"

"Yes, Elfrida—and your husband. I won't keep you long. Let's get in out of this."

The "shall we?" he added was purely perfunctory. He took her arm, steered her back around the corner, down steps and on into the Rockingham cocktail lounge. The smart black and white lamplit room wasn't crowded. The storm was probably keeping people away. She and Harvey dropped in here occasionally. Dace looked around but there was no one she knew in sight. Not, she told herself, that it made the slightest difference. Hugh walked her to a dim recess and she sat down on the banquette and pulled off her gloves. Hugh sat facing her. Her hands were pink with cold and she slammed them softly together to bring the blood back.

Harvey had seen Elfrida yesterday; had they quarreled about something then? Harvey hadn't said anything. . . . But Hugh Clavering was in Elfrida's confidence, she was very fond of him—and Hugh was unlike his usual self, he was preoccupied, aloof, with no spark. She looked at him sitting across the table from her, ordering from the waiter; at his lean, dark face, the arrogant tilt of his head, his mouth, his eyes; and without the slightest warning

18

gladness welled up in her. It was as if some deep hunger and thirst in her that she had denied, refused to recognize, was being satisfied. She couldn't help this. It was completely involuntary, the only thing she could do was to push it away, hide it, bury it out of sight. It was probably because she was distressed and nervously upset; it was simply an automatic ghost of other, happier days in which she was seeking refuge. That was all.

Hugh lit her cigarette and his own, the waiter brought their drinks, and when he was gone Hugh told her.

Dace looked at him and then away, her hands gripping the edge of the table. "No," she cried, staring sightlessly at a bank of colored bottles behind the bar. "Oh, no." She couldn't breathe. The knot of fur at her throat was strangling her. She loosened the scarf and pulled it off.

Harvey had forged a check on Elfrida's account for a thousand dollars and had signed Elfrida's name to it.

"I'm afraid he did." Hugh went on making circles on the black table top with the bottom of his glass.

Dace looked at the circles, there were four of them and then there were five. . . . It was impossible. . . . Harvey might do crazy things sometimes, but not anything like this . . . Forgery! Forgery was a crime. Harvey was impetuous, headlong, a creature of impulse, and once he got an idea in his head, determined to have his way come hell or high water. But he was not a criminal. Nor was he insane, and to try and get away with a check for a thousand dollars, particularly with a woman like Elfrida Allert, would be insanity.

She moistened lips as dry as the Sahara. "I—don't believe it, Hugh. There must be some mistake. I can't believe it. It *can't* be true."

But even as she spoke sureness began to dwindle. The thousand dollars in Harvey's wallet, the tale of a winning horse, his early return from the office that day, his proposal that they get out of New York instantly, that afternoon . . .

Hugh was talking, quietly. She forced herself to listen.

The check was made out to Harvey and signed with Elfrida's name. Harvey's endorsement was on the back. He had cashed the check early that morning. Under ordinary circumstances it might have taken days, weeks,

19

for the fraud to be uncovered, but a bank official who knew Elfrida personally and who also knew Harvey, saw Harvey going out and took a look at the check. He became suspicious and called Elfrida at her hotel. She had called Harvey at his office.

Snow struck the windows above their heads with soft violence. "What did Harvey say?"

Hugh swirled ice in his glass, studied the pattern the cubes made. "That's the point, that's the bad part of it, Dace. Harvey denied it. He told Elfrida the check had come in the morning mail and he thought she had sent it to him because she knew he was pressed for cash—they had talked about it yesterday at the hotel. He didn't hem and haw, he acknowledged cashing the check without any hesitation at all, swore that he thought it was genuine. But . . ."

Hugh put a light to a fresh cigarette and looked past Dace. His expression was enough. Without his going on she understood all that he didn't say. Who but Harvey would forge Elfrida's name to a check for a thousand dollars? Who else would do such a thing and then send the check to Harvey as largess, an entertaining prank, for fun? Doubts that had been shredding away bit by bit died dreadfully. There was no winning horse. . . . Harvey had lied, he must have . . .

Music was playing softly somewhere. A woman laughed. The bartender made a noise with a cocktail shaker. "What is Elfrida going to do?"

Hugh had been giving her time. He looked at her then searchingly. There was approval in his eyes. He nodded and drank some of his Scotch.

"That's why I wanted to see you. Elfrida's very upset, and very angry. It was Harvey's denial that made her so furious. She says he's got to be stopped now, given a jolt that will teach him a lesson. She's making all sorts of threats but—wait a minute, Dace—I think, I'm practically sure, that if she's handled the right way, that's all it will be —threats. I tried to talk to her. It wasn't any use, she wouldn't listen to me. But I'm positive that if Harvey appeals to her, if he tells her the truth and returns the money and throws himself on her mercy, she'll come

20

round. Only it ought to be done right away, before she does anything, takes any steps . . ."

He paused, hesitated, and went on, "If Harvey hasn't got the thousand, if it's already gone, I can . . ."

Dace stopped him. She was sick with shock and humiliation and shame. There was nothing in her experience to guide her. Forgery . . . It was such a mean crime, deliberate, cunning, sly—altogether vile. And Harvey had done this, the man she had married. Hugh Clavering's offer of help was kind—and indescribably bitter.

She said crisply, "Thanks, Hugh, but it won't be necessary. Harvey has the thousand. Elfrida's not in New York still, is she?"

Hugh said no, that she had left the hotel at around three for the farm in Duchess County. He glanced at his watch. "She ought to be up there now." He studied Dace's face. "Don't take it so hard—it isn't too late. If you can make Harvey see reason, convince him that Elfrida means business, that she's in earnest, everything will come out all right. I tried to tell him but . . ." He shrugged, and sat back in his chair.

Dace was startled. "You saw Harvey, Hugh?"

He nodded. "Yes, I saw him."

"When?"

"A little while ago. I went to your house. You were the one I wanted to see but you weren't there."

Dace knocked a long ash from her cigarette. Hugh's face and voice were expressionless; the warmth had gone out of him. What had happened between him and Harvey? They had never been particularly friendly and in the mood Harvey was in . . . Had they quarreled? She didn't ask. A feeling of urgency was gathering in her. Enough time had gone by as it was. She had to talk to Harvey and get hold of the money and call Elfrida. . . . She picked up her sable scarf, tightened it around her throat. "I'd better go," she said.

"Yes," Hugh agreed soberly, but he didn't move. He was looking at her again, steadily, searchingly. His eyes were no longer bleak, aloof. "Dace—are you happy?"

Dace knew very well what he meant. He was asking her

21

whether her marriage was a success. He wasn't entitled to do that, to ask any such question. His wife was dead and he was free; she wasn't. Against her will it seemed as though Hugh could still make her forget it. . . . Anger came to her aid, anger at herself and her own response, involuntary or not. She ignored the real meaning of his question. She said dryly, "Well I can't say that at the moment I feel exactly like throwing up my hat and giving three cheers," and gathered her purse and gloves and rose.

Hugh sat eyeing her thoughtfully for a moment, then got up and pulled the table out for her. "I'll see you home."

"No," she told him, "it's only a step. Good-bye, Hugh—and thanks." She held out her hand.

He took it in his and they looked at each other. There was nothing more that could be said by either of them, nothing. She withdrew her hand and turned quickly away.

The room was filling up and the bar was already crowded. Moving between the tables Dace's thoughts were chaotic, confused; she was glad she wasn't going to have to face anyone she knew. She was mistaken. She hadn't gone more than ten feet when she was hailed.

"Dace—Dace Allert."

It was Harvey's cousin Joan Longstreet who blocked her path. Joan was a tall, broad-shouldered woman in her early forties, always superlatively well-dressed, with an excellent figure, a great many white teeth, round blue eyes, and a well-taken-care-of skin, the girlish type, eager, frank, ingenuous, and oh, so charming and anxious to please. Actually she was a highly paid executive in a top-flight advertising agency.

"Darling, how *nice*. You look *wonderful*." She greeted Dace as though she were the one person in the world she most wanted to see, as though it filled her cup of happiness to the brim. "I didn't know you were here."

She smiled her bright, empty smile and flashed her teeth. Then her gaze left Dace and moved to the embrasure where Hugh Clavering sat alone at the table holding two glasses and the red-tipped cigarette Dace had left in the ash tray.

She turned back to the younger woman with the shadow

22

of a smile, a coy, meaningful smile. "Isn't that—Hugh Clavering, Dace?"

"It is."

"I didn't know he was in New York."

There was nothing to say to that so Dace didn't say it. Joan Longstreet's table was fairly near theirs. How long had she been there? Could she have overheard them talking? It was extremely unlikely. Music was playing softly and the murmur of voices was a steady hum. Besides, Joan adored Harvey and if she had heard about the check she wouldn't look so calm. The answer to that was fast—Joan Longstreet would look calm and composed in the middle of a cyclone or a rescue at sea if it suited her purposes to do so. She went on burbling sweetly with words that were seldom more than a cover for other and different thoughts. She said she was waiting for her husband. The storm had probably delayed Kermit. . . . Wasn't it frightful . . . ? They thought of dropping around to the house later on, after dinner, there was something Kermit wanted to see Harvey about.

Dace put her off. A pity—but she and Harvey were going out. She refused a sherry, "I can't Joan, dear, I've got to run," and made her escape.

Wind seized her the moment she stepped out on the pavement. The visibility was practically nonexistent. Snow blew from every direction. It was almost sleet. Tiny pellets hit Dace's cheeks and forehead stingingly. The cold was intense. She scarcely felt the icy drive. Now that she was alone the full horror of Harvey and the forged check had its way with her. Guilt was what had been at the bottom of Harvey's rage that afternoon, guilt and fear . . . How could he have done such a thing, how could he?—and yet he had. His only idea had been to put plenty of distance between himself and New York and the consequences of the forged check. . . . She had to convince him that he couldn't run away, that he would have to stay and face up to what he had done. Suppose he refused to, suppose he stuck to his lie about receiving the check in the mail? What then? He wouldn't, couldn't—not when she told him that Elfrida intended to go to the police unless he admitted the truth.

23

She fought her way down the block to the tall iron gate, through it and along the narrow passage just wide enough for the car between two towering apartment houses, and into the open where the little hidden court widened out. In summer it was green and leafy and cool in dappled sunshine and shadow after the glare of the streets; now there was nothing to be seen but the faint glimmer of the lantern beside the door with the numerals 234A set in the brick under it. She mounted the low steps and fitted her key into the lock. Her fingers were numb. There seemed to be something wrong. . . . Then she got the door open and closed it behind her, shutting out the bitter air and a swish of whirling snow.

The hall was quiet in lamplight. White and russet chrysanthemums bloomed stirlessly against the green gold of the wall with the slim, graceful staircase rising on the right. Everything about the house was small but in perfect proportion. She stamped snow from her feet on the black and white marble floor, brushed it from her coat, shook her fur scarf and put them in the closet. There was no sound of voices, no sound anywhere. Where was Olivia? Hugh had said she was here. Perhaps she had waited and then given it up and gone home on account of the storm. Perhaps the storm was keeping Gerald Straws away. She hoped so. She had to talk to Harvey alone.

Neither the radio nor the television was on. Under ordinary circumstances Harvey invariably played one or the other from the moment he came in until they went to bed, whether he listened or not. The circumstances weren't ordinary. He had put up a bluff with her that afternoon but when he was alone bluff would fail him. Where was he? Dreading the task of confronting him she walked slowly toward the living room and paused in the doorway. The silvery green satin curtains were drawn across the windows, lamps bloomed in the corners. Polished wood, the dado of books vivid against the pale apricot walls, the unlit fire; Harvey wasn't there. He was probably upstairs. She was turning away when she saw the brief case.

It was lying on the coffee table in front of the couch. She crossed the room. The initials on the tan leather were

24

K.C.L.—Kermit Cass Longstreet. The brief case belonged to Joan Longstreet's husband.

Kermit was probably upstairs with Harvey; her throat ached with pinpricks of frustration, annoyed impatience. Someone else to get rid of, another obstacle to clear out of the way before she could get to grips with Harvey and what had to be done and done quickly.

Kermit Longstreet wasn't upstairs with Harvey. As she was leaving the room the doorbell rang and she answered it, and Kermit came in out of the snow.

He was a tall, thin man in his early fifties with half-blond, half-gray hair receding from the temples of a pleasant, weather-beaten face, rather sweet—and very much under his wife's thumb. His thralldom was a perpetual wonder to Dace: he was much more intelligent than Joan and yet he deferred to her in everything, seemed to think she was the font of all wisdom. He and Dace had liked each other instinctively from the first, and as always, Kermit's greeting was warm, friendly.

"Hello, Dace, my dear, how are you? You're looking well. Phew—some storm—at this time of year, too. Looks as though we're in for a bad winter."

He had come for his brief case. He was a corporation lawyer and there were valuable papers in it. He couldn't stay. . . . Joan was waiting for him around at the Rockingham bar. "Harvey back yet?" he asked.

"Back?" Dace said, startled.

"Yes. There was no one here when I walked in a little while ago. The door was on the latch and there wasn't a soul around—not, by the way, a very wise thing to leave the door like that in New York. I waited a couple of minutes and shouted—began to feel as though I'd boarded the *Marie-Celeste*. Harvey must have stepped out for cigarettes or something and left the door unlocked."

That was why she had trouble with her key. To Dace's relief Kermit went immediately. He was late as it was and Joan would be having fits, she was dying of hunger. The Longstreets lived in Croton and Kermit was anxious to get home before the roads got any worse. He said he wanted a word with Harvey, but it wasn't too important and he'd give him a ring tomorrow. He had scarcely gone and Dace was starting for the stairs when the bell rang again. This time it was her cousin, Olivia Wood, and it was Olivia who had left the door on the latch.

She came in with a rush in a fresh shower of snow. At the sight of Dace she gave a sigh of relief. "Thank heavens you're here, Dace," she exclaimed. "I was worried to death. . . . I had visions of all sorts of things, your furs, your jewelry gone, maybe the furniture moved out . . ."

Olivia's skin was pink with cold and her eyes big and dark. The white wool scarf over her head made her look like a tall madonna; she was a very pretty girl. She had been in the house earlier, quite some time ago. Harvey had let her in, and then she had discovered that she had forgotten to mail some important letters her boss had given her when she left the office. Harvey had gone upstairs and she didn't want to bother him, which was why she had left the door on the latch.

She said, "I thought I'd only be a minute but I walked blocks and blocks before I found a postbox. I must have passed dozens, but you know me without my glasses, blind as a bat, and I simply couldn't wear them, they kept getting plastered with snow." She took them out of her pocket, polished them on a fold of her red cardigan that burned gaily in the soft light, and put them on. "There, that's better. Now I can see."

Dace looked at her cousin attentively. Olivia was talking too much and too fast, and she was not a chatterer. Also she was uneasy and nervous, and trying hard to hide it. Harvey was very fond of her, but in the mood he was in . . . Had he said something, done something . . . ?

Dace said, "Olivia, what is it, what's the matter?"

At the mirror Olivia was running her fingers through her short brown curls, patting them into place. She turned slowly. Her big eyes searched Dace's face.

"Didn't Harvey tell you?"

"I haven't seen him, I only just got in."

"Well, Hugh Clavering was here and—he and Harvey had a fight."

"A fight? You mean an actual . . ."

"Yes." Olivia nodded solemnly. She said that Harvey

26

and Hugh Clavering had tried to beat each other up. She had gone upstairs to fix her face. Starting down again she had heard the rumpus from the top of the stairs. Then it stopped and Hugh Clavering came out of the living room into the hall. "He asked where you were, Dace. I told him I didn't know but I was sure you'd be in soon, and he went."

She said that when she got into the living room Harvey was there picking himself up off the floor. Except for a cut lip he wasn't hurt. A chair had been knocked over, and the fire tongs. "Harvey didn't say anything, but he was pretty furious." Olivia shook her head. "He just sort of looked through me as though I wasn't there, then he walked off and went upstairs. That's why I didn't want to disturb him, why I left the door . . ."

She broke off, staring. "Dace—for goodness *sakes* . . . The sky hasn't fallen. Harvey's got a quick temper and he wasn't in a good mood when I first came and he let me in. It was probably nothing at all—some stupid argument they got into."

Fortunately Olivia wasn't a girl who asked inconvenient questions. Dace had never been able to determine whether this lack of curiosity was due to discretion or the disinterest of a child in what it can't see, touch, taste, hear or feel. But civilized men didn't go at each other hammer and tongs over nothing. It was the check, of course. Harvey couldn't bear Hugh Clavering's knowing about the check and he had exploded. . . . "Yes," she said, "Yes, I suppose it was something like that. . . . I'll go upstairs and see Harvey, see if he's all right."

Harvey wasn't in the big bedroom adjoining hers on the floor above, he wasn't in the game room on the third floor, he wasn't anywhere in the house.

The money, Dace thought distractedly, the thousand dollars that had to be returned to Elfrida . . . Harvey might have gone to the club, might get into a game . . . Suppose he lost the thousand? There were no reserves to fall back on. There was only a couple of hundred in the bank and there wouldn't be any more for two weeks. And there were the maids to be paid and the house to run. . . . And Hugh had stressed haste. . . . What was she to do?

27

How was she to talk to Elfrida? What could she say?

Another fear rose in her as she started getting out of her wet things in her own bedroom. Harvey must have gone out after Olivia left to post her letters and before Kermit Longstreet came. Could he have followed Hugh Clavering, could he have seen them meet near the gate and go around to the Rockingham bar together? If so, it would deepen his rage. . . .

She shrugged impatiently. Harvey and Hugh Clavering were both grown men—and anyhow there was nothing she could do about that. Elfrida was the important one. She had to do something about Elfrida, and do it fast. The best thing to do was to call Elfrida at the farm, try and gauge her mood, and say that Harvey had been held up by the storm and would ring her later. If Hugh had been right, if he had sized up Elfrida correctly, this would stop her from doing anything about the check in the meantime. Dace picked up the phone.

Madge Tarbel, an old friend of Elfrida's who lived with her as a companion, answered. Dace liked Madge, whom she knew better than she did Elfrida; Madge had stayed with them last year when Elfrida was abroad and Harvey was laid up with neuritis. She was a woman in her sixties, calm and kind and as easy as an old shoe. She had been wonderful with Harvey, making him laugh and keeping him contented and in a good humor.

After she talked to Madge for a moment Dace asked for Elfrida, and Madge said she wasn't at the farm, that she hadn't arrived yet, she was stopping off to see friends in Eastbrook on the way up. Dace said, "Will you tell her I called, Madge, and that it's rather urgent, and ask her to ring me as soon as she gets in. I'll be here all evening."

Madge said she would and Dace hung up and went on dressing quickly. Harvey mightn't have gone to the club, he might come back any minute, and she wanted to be there when he came in. On her way to the door she encountered her image in the full-length mirror. She had thrown on the first thing her hand had encountered in the wardrobe, and the unrelieved black sheath made her look like Mary, Queen of Scots on her way to the scaffold.

There was no use advertising the fact in advance to Olivia and Gerald Straws that there was anything wrong—if Gerald came. Surely if Elfrida got the money back and Harvey ate plenty of crow, that would be the end of this terrible business. She went back to the dressing table and put on the little string of pearls Elfrida had given her on her marriage and used rouge and more lipstick. They weren't much help but they were better than nothing.

Harvey wasn't there when she got downstairs; Olivia was alone in the living room placidly sipping a drink and reading a magazine. Harvey wasn't at the club, either—Dace called there. Well anyhow, that was something to the good—his gambling away the thousand dollars was what she feared most.

It was his continued absence that gave her a cover for the stress she couldn't completely hide; not from Olivia who knew her too well, or from Gerald Straws when Gerald finally came—he had phoned to say he'd be late. Olivia had taken the call or Dace would have told him not to come.

Although Gerald Straws was one of Harvey's oldest friends—they had known each other since prep school—no two men could have been more completely different. Harvey was outgoing, gregarious, and at heart deeply conventional. Gerald was calm, steady and cool-headed, and didn't give a damn for anyone's opinion but his own, which for the most part he kept to himself—and he cared nothing whatever about appearances. When Harvey railed at his clothes—"Where did you pick up that suit, on the Bowery?"—Gerald would say, "What's the matter with it, I don't see anything wrong," and smile his lazy smile.

That night Gerald Straws saw right away that there was something wrong. As soon as he came in he asked where Harvey was and when Dace said, "I don't know. He was here late this afternoon, he let Olivia in, but when I got back at a little before six he was gone," Gerald gave her a keen look, brows raised over the luminous light eyes that were too perceptive by far.

"One of his moods?" he asked, sauntering toward the fire and tossing a handful of salted peanuts into his mouth.

Dace nodded. "A bit."

29

"And I suppose you tried to argue with him?"

His tone was humorous but Dace could feel her color rising. It was none of Gerald's business. He might be Harvey's friend but she was Harvey's wife, a fact he sometimes seemed to forget.

He went on eyeing her. "Fireworks?" She shrugged and he looked away, looked at the mantel. "Hello—what became of the ginger jar?"

Dace was tired of dodging. She said, "Harvey threw it on the floor this afternoon," and Gerald whistled, but he frowned at the same time. "He must have had steam up for fair. . . . He's probably bending his elbow somewhere. . . ." He looked at her again. "What's eating you, lovie?"

That was it, Dace thought. It was this sort of thing that made Harvey sore. Gerald was simply amusing himself but Harvey resented it because it took Gerald's attention away from him, and he was as jealous as any woman. . . . She couldn't talk about the check to anyone. It was too dreadful.

She said, "I *am* edgy—the storm, I guess. The snow's pretty bad, and if Harvey should get tight . . ."

"Nonsense." Gerald took out his pipe. "Harvey knows his way around and if he's under the weather he'll hole up somewhere for the night."

"But if he'd only let me *know* . . ."

Gerald smiled amiably. "Use your head, Dace. To hear you anyone would think this was the first time. Wasn't it last Easter that he took off for the Gaspé without a word to a soul? He was gone a week then. He'll come back when he's simmered down. Stop worrying."

Was there irony in his admonition? She gave him a cool stare. Olivia missed the nuances between them. She was openly indignant.

"It's easy to say don't worry. I'm as fond of Harvey as anybody, but I don't know how you *stand* things like this, Dace. Stalking out in a senseless rage—I swear if he were my husband I'd kill him. You ought to give him a taste of his own medicine, give him a scare, walk out yourself sometime."

Gerald grinned at her vehemence. "Whoa up, young one. Give the lad a chance. He may stroll in at any moment."

But Harvey didn't stroll in. The maids had left things ready so the three of them had some drinks and a scratch meal on a table in front of the fire—and Dace's anxiety grew. Not only did Harvey not come in but Elfrida didn't phone. Perhaps, on account of the storm, she had decided to stay the night with the people she had stopped in to see on her way up to the farm. In that case she would have let Madge Tarbel know. Dace rang Madge but there was no answer. The couple who ran the farm lived in a cottage some distance from the big house and Dace knew neither their name nor their number. She gave it up. There was nothing to do now but wait.

They were having coffee when Gerald said suddenly in the middle of talk about something else, "What about your car, Dace?"

The Benz was in a garage not far away. Dace said, "I don't know," and Gerald went to the phone. He came back frowning. Harvey had the car. He had phoned the garage late in the afternoon and a man had brought the Benz around and parked it in the court at the side of the house at about twenty minutes past four. He had delivered the keys to Harvey in person.

Snow that was almost sleet kept striking at the windows behind the drawn curtains. The wind blew. You could hear the rise and fall of it. Olivia said, "Oh, dear," and took off her glasses and wiped them. Gerald said firmly, "Oh, dear—nonsense. Harvey's a hell of a good driver—and anyhow he's probably undercover somewhere taking his ease." They both looked at Dace.

Dace didn't look at either of them, she looked into the fire. They didn't know, but she did. Earlier in the day Harvey had wanted her to leave New York and she had refused, so he had gone by himself. He was running away from the check and its consequences—from Elfrida. It was a natural reaction, the way his mind worked. Turn your back on unpleasantness, difficulties; refuse to look at them and they disappear. It was what he did with bills. She agonized over them; he tore them up blithely and threw them into the trashbasket. The check was much more serious, but he didn't seem to realize it. . . .

Gerald went before ten. He remained determinedly calm and cheerful. It was no use hanging around; there

31

was nothing useful he could do and he had a couple of heavy days coming up. He had to drive to Albany tomorrow. Both of them ought to go to bed early. "You look worn out, Dace, though I can't understand why. It isn't as though you weren't used to this sort of shenanigan."

He had scarcely gone when the phone rang.

It wasn't Harvey. It was Madge Tarbel. Dace listened, and froze. Elfrida had had an accident in her car. She was in a hospital near Fishkill and wasn't expected to live the night.

THREE

That was all that Dace was told that evening in New York. On the scene where the accident occurred, some sixty odd miles to the north—one of a countless number blamed on the storm—the usual examination had taken place hours earlier. Elfrida Allert had crashed at shortly before four o'clock in the afternoon, and the state police highway patrol car was on the scene within minutes, sent there by a passing motorist. The car Mrs. Allert had been driving was a complete wreck, and she herself was pinned behind the wheel in an apparently dying condition. An ambulance and a doctor arrived shortly thereafter and Elfrida Allert was removed to the nearest hospital. One of the troopers rode in the ambulance with her in case she should recover consciousness. The other trooper stayed where he was.

What had happened was clear enough. The road there, a narrow, winding, secondary road, swung in a sharp curve around the flank of a hill. Snow was beginning to pile up and the surface was bad. Either the injured woman had approached the curve too fast or the car had gone out of control through a mechanical fault; there was no question of a collision with another vehicle. The Torshe-Hamton had slammed into one of a pair of heavy stone pillars leading to a driveway, with terrific force. The whole front end of the car was telescoped, the engine driven back into the body. The shatterproof glass didn't actually break but there wasn't an inch of it that didn't look like white blotting paper.

Photographs were taken and then the car was towed away. Elfrida Allert's identity had been established on the scene through the driving license in her purse and other papers. The address on the license was Stony Hill Road, Silverbridge, New York. The number was in the book. The receiving nurse at the hospital put a call through to the house but there was no answer.

Mrs. Allert was obviously a wealthy woman, the mink coat she wore was a beauty and there were valuable rings on her fingers; the doctors gathered in force. There was very little they could do, the patient was thoroughly smashed up. There were head and internal injuries, a broken pelvis and compound fractures of both legs and one arm. If by some miracle she did manage to survive she would be a hopeless cripple. Mercifully she hadn't regained consciousness, probably wouldn't regain consciousness before she died.

The switchboard girl kept trying to reach the dying woman's home in Silverbridge at intervals throughout the late afternoon and early evening. She finally got hold of a Miss Madge Tarbel at the Duchess County farm at shortly before nine P.M.

Elfrida Allert didn't die that night. She was still alive, but just barely, the next morning. In the house in the court on Murray Hill, her mind in turmoil, Dace waited for the news of Elfrida's death and for Harvey to come back. In spite of herself the tensions in her had eased a little. What had happened to Elfrida was terrible and shocking. She was saddened, profoundly sorry and distressed, but she had never known the older woman well and she had no sense of personal grief or loss. It was impossible to help her feeling of relief that Harvey was safe. Nothing could or would be done about the check now, unless Elfrida had done something before she left New York. From what Hugh Clavering had said, that was extremely unlikely.

Olivia had spent the night with Dace but she had gone to work and Dace wandered around the house unable to

34

settle to anything. She had looked in Harvey's room last night but she looked again, more carefully. Harvey had gone out in the gray suit he had worn to the office and his dark blue vicuña overcoat. He hadn't taken any personal things with him; his shaving gear, brushes, even his toothbrush, were all there in place. Pushing things around on the rack in the wardrobe, she noticed the smear of grease on the sleeve of his tan tweed ulster. He had got that when he was tinkering with Elfrida's car; she had noticed it at the time. She started to take it out to drop at the cleaners, and shoved it back. She wasn't going out anywhere.

There was nothing about Elfrida in the papers, although they were full of the damage the storm had done, wires down, homes darkened, electricity and phones out of commission and a number of deaths attributed directly or indirectly to the wind and the heavy, clinging snow. Harvey wouldn't learn about Elfrida that way.

He hadn't turned up at the office—she was sure he wouldn't—but she had tried there anyhow. A girl's voice simply said that, no, Mr. Allert hadn't come in. After that she rang five or six people with whom Harvey might have stayed the night, without result. And then, at three o'clock in the afternoon, she had word at last. But before that Harvey's cousin Joan Longstreet called her.

The memory of the little scene in the Rockingham bar late the afternoon before and a million miles in the past was both vivid and unpleasant to Dace. Joan's blue eyes, wide with surprise and something else, going to the table where Hugh Clavering sat, returning to her face measuringly, no doubt absorbing the evidences of the shock she had had at what Hugh told her about Elfrida and the forged check. Joan didn't like her and never had. There was probably nothing personal in it. She wouldn't have liked any woman Harvey married; she had always adored him, and under her sweet amiability she was both jealous and possessive. According to kind friends, Joan laid their money difficulties at Dace's door with a shake of her hand and a worried smile. "Poor darling Harvey, I'm afraid that wife of his is no manager, and she's so terribly extravagant. It would make the hair stand up on your head . . ."

If Harvey couldn't find out from the papers, neither could Joan; it was evident that she didn't know about Elfrida.

She asked brightly about Sunday night and the Berisfords. Had Dace spoken to Harvey, and could she count on them both? Dace said vaguely, "The Berisfords?" and Joan said yes. "Don't you remember?—I mentioned it to you yesterday in the Rockingham."

Dace contemplated her nails. Joan's implication was that she had been too upset at being discovered with Hugh Clavering to recall anything. . . . She was waiting for an answer. Dace had no intention of telling her about Harvey and the check. Temporize.

"No, Joan, I didn't speak to Harvey, didn't get around to it, he had to go away."

"Away?" Joan was surprised and persistent. "Away where, darling?"

Dace snatched at the first thing that presented itself. It had happened a couple of weeks ago and they hadn't seen the Longstreets since. She said, "You remember Tony Milstrom, don't you? Harvey was always so fond of him. . . . Well, Tony's ill, jaundice or something, and Harvey drove up to see him."

"You mean Harvey took the car out yesterday in that storm. . . . And you let him? Oh, Dace . . ."

Choke her off, Dace thought, I've got to tell her about Elfrida anyhow. She did, and it was more than effective.

Joan was stunned. For a moment she was completely speechless. Then she got her breath. Elfrida injured in a car accident and not expected to live? How terrible, how perfectly frightful—poor, poor creature. A barrage of questions—when had it happened? How? Did Harvey know, had Dace gotten in touch with him? Where did Tony Milstrom live?

Dace said that beyond the fact that it was somewhere up in eastern New York State past Albany she had no idea, but that Harvey would be calling her soon anyhow and that she would tell him about Elfrida then.

Joan was dissatisfied. Harvey ought to be told at once. He would probably want to go to Elfrida. It was going to make a terrific difference. . . . There would be endless things for him to do. Dace ought to try and get hold of him immediately, without the loss of a minute. The Milstroms' address must be somewhere in the house. Dace could put in a person-to-person call. . . . "Perhaps I'd better come down, dear."

Dace was suddenly tired of Joan, and of the covert exultation in her at the change in Harvey's prospects. She said, "No, Joan, don't come, I've got to go out."

"But if Harvey calls you . . ."

Dace said firmly, "The maids are here, and in any case I won't be long," and hung up.

After that, for the next hour, the phone rang almost continuously. The queen is dead—or as good as—long live the king. Kermit Longstreet called, and various other friends of theirs Joan had promptly informed. . . . Spread the good news. But not Harvey. Nothing from Harvey. And then, at a little after four, Irene Branch rang Dace.

The Branches were a pleasant couple with four children who lived in a big, old-fashioned house on the banks of the Hudson above Hastings. Jim Branch worked in Harvey's office. Dace liked them both.

Irene Branch said, "What gives with that husband of yours, Dace? He called the office this morning and said he wouldn't be in and Jim thought he was sick, but when I got home from collecting the kids at dancing school, Clarissa—that's my daily—told me that Harvey had called me here. He said he was in town and wanted to see me. That was a couple of hours ago and I've been waiting in ever since, but no Harvey. There's nothing—wrong, is there?"

Dace pulled air into her lungs and let it out in a long sigh. It was the first deep breath she had drawn in almost twenty-four hours. Hastings wasn't very far away. It would take Harvey less than an hour to get home from there. Irene was a soft, pretty woman, kind and sympathetic, and he might have gone to her for comfort. . . . Dace thought remorsefully, perhaps I am too hard. Can a jackanapes be merry? There were plenty of occasions when she must be a clog at Harvey's heels. . . . She could be frank with Irene.

She said, "There's nothing wrong except that we had a word or two yesterday afternoon and Harvey was upset, you know the way he gets, and he walked out and I haven't seen him since. He may be on his way home by now, but if he does go to your place, tell him to call me right away, will you?"

Irene said she would and that she understood perfectly. Men were wonderful but they took a lot of handling. When Jim got into one of his sulks it sometimes lasted for days. He had walked out on her the other night and gone to the movies because she had served shoestring potatoes three times in one week. "And I thought he liked them."

After Irene rang off Dace wandered restlessly around the living room, plumping the green satin cushions on the love seat, rearranging a clump of white carnations, pausing at the window to look out at the snow-covered cobbles and the backs of houses beyond the fence. No, she needn't have been so cool, so curt with Harvey yesterday when he came in whistling nervously. If only he had told her about the check then, everything would have been different. The heinousness of what he had done was dimmer now, less vivid. It was wrong, yes, but in some twisted way Harvey looked on the Allert money as his own. . . . And the check was in the past, done with, wasn't it? If only there was someone she could talk to, who would set her nagging fear at rest . . . The counselor who presently came was not only unwelcome; the result of his visit was disastrous. At half past four Mr. Charles Beecham arrived at the house.

Charles Beecham was the senior partner of Beecham, Gantz and Perfield, the law firm that handled Elfrida's affairs. Dace had never met him but even without his introduction of himself she would have recognized him from Harvey's description. "An enormous fat white rat, with claws—eighteen feet tall. Give you the willies."

Beecham did remind one of a rat, an immense one. He was in his fifties, and large in every direction, with an impressive bald head and brilliantly polished glasses with a black ribbon trailing away from them. Gertrude showed him in and retreated and Beecham took Dace's hand as though it were a rare jewel. At first she thought he was going to raise it to his lips but he merely bowed low over it.

Mrs. Allert . . . A pleasure . . . A pity the occasion was so sad. He had been in touch with the hospital on and off all day. He had known Elfrida for many years, charming, charming, altogether delightful, and, as age went now, with a life expectancy of another two decades. A tragedy. The police were investigating. Nothing was known definitely yet, but the car must have been defective, some essential part must have failed. It was comparatively new and he was of the opinion that a suit would lie . . . He had sent a man of his own up there to look into things. Meanwhile, umm, yes—now he would like to see Harvey.

Dace said Harvey wasn't there, the lurking fear in her gathering force. Before she left New York on her fatal drive had Elfrida talked to this man, or hadn't she? Charles Beecham was her lawyer and it would be natural for her to consult him; she hadn't hesitated to talk freely to Hugh Clavering about the forged check. There was nothing to be gathered from Beecham's manner. He remained urbane.

Ah well, he had hoped to catch Harvey at this hour. . . . He should have telephoned but he thought he would just stop by on his way uptown. Of course Harvey would have things to do. . . . However, the sooner they got together, the better—in affairs of this kind forewarned was forearmed. The estate was large and there were always things pending. Elfrida's death could only be a matter of hours. . . . Dace understood the situation?

She nodded. "On his stepmother's death Harvey inherits everything."

"Quite right."

Dace was watching Beecham closely and it seemed to her as though a veil drew itself across the large, inscrutable face and the hidden eyes. Nothing confronted her but the brilliantly shining glasses, uninformative and scrutinizing. . . . A nameless fear took hold of her. It had nothing to do with the check, it was something in the man himself, some deadly threat that sprang out of nowhere, for no reason . . . She pushed panic down. It was her nerves, imagination, strain . . . Find out about the check right now.

She ran a forefinger over a dusting of gold in the ivory wood of the armchair in which she sat, and raised her eyes. "Did you see Elfrida when she was in New York this last time, Mr. Beecham?"

He shook his massive head sadly. "Alas, no. But we had a long chat over the telephone."

You could tell nothing whatever from his manner. If he did know about the check why didn't he speak out? Mr. Charles Beecham would never speak out—in under a hundred pages of a carefully considered brief, produced when it suited him to do so. The house was very still, the noise of distant traffic muted by snow. A jolt went through Dace. Outside in the hall there was a faint sound. Was it the front door opening and closing? Was it Harvey?

For no good reason she had a passionate desire that Harvey shouldn't come in while Beecham was there. Harvey was impetuous, he didn't like the man and he wouldn't scruple to show his feelings, he never did—and Beecham would be a bad enemy. She listened without moving. The sound had been faint. Perhaps Beecham hadn't heard it—but he had.

He broke off what he was starting to say, turned his head and looked expectantly toward the hall. "Perhaps that's your husband now."

"Oh?" Dace got up and crossed the floor. But it wasn't Harvey. It wasn't anyone. Tranquil in lamplight the hall was empty and untenanted, and the front door firmly closed. Queer that both she and Beecham had heard that sound . . . Of course, she thought with sudden relief, it was probably Gertrude coming upstairs for something.

Beecham stayed another twenty minutes, talking about nothing in mellifluous phrases, and studying her as though he were making a précis, age, height, eyes, skin, weight, temperament, capabilities. He asked about Gerald Straws. "I used to see a lot of Straws when Harvey's father was alive; he was fond of Straws." Then he spoke of Hugh Clavering. He had been swinging the glasses to and fro on the black ribbon, he planted them on his big nose. "You know Clavering, Mrs. Allert?"

Careful, Dace thought, careful. She said, "Oh, yes," and Beecham said it was a pity he and Elfrida's niece Dolly had never had any children, now there would be no one of Elfrida's own blood left. This was a non sequitur as far as Dace could see. Presently Beecham got on the subject of wills. If he might ask, if it wasn't impertinent,

40

but under the circumstances—"You and your husband have taken care of that?"

Dace said yes, at the time of their marriage.

"Good. Good." At long last Beecham finally rose. He wanted very much to talk to Harvey, very much indeed.

The fear again, nameless, formless. Dace said Harvey would call him first thing in the morning, and the lawyer went.

He was only just gone when Olivia got back. She came in looking radiant and carefree, her cheeks rosy with cold. Pulling off her gray astrakhan cap, she ran her fingers through her curls.

"Thank God, Dace," she exclaimed. "You must be *so* relieved. What did he say?"

Dace stared at her blankly. "Who? What do you mean?"

It was Olivia's turn to stare. "Who? Why Harvey, of course. Your car's parked out there on Thirty-seventh Street just beyond the gate. Harvey's back, isn't he?"

FOUR

It was dark out and bitterly cold. But there was light enough from the street lamp a little farther along to see by. The Benz was there, parked beyond the gates, between a truck and the fire plug, just as Olivia 'had said. It was theirs. There was no one in it and the doors were locked. Dace put a hand on the radiator. It was still faintly warm. It must have been Harvey who had come into the house while she was with Beecham in the living room. . . . She looked up and down the dim street. Figures in the distance, hurrying along through the winter darkness, a woman running with a wirehair and a dachshund, four or five men at intervals; none of them Harvey.

Coldness struck through the thin soles of Dace's pumps. She gathered folds of the coat she had thrown on tighter around her, turned away and retraced her steps. The alley was empty in darkness. So was the entire court.

When she went in Olivia was down on one knee putting a match to the living-room fire. She turned an anxious face.

"Well?"

Dace sat down slowly in a chair close to the hearth. The coldness stayed in her, she couldn't seem to get warm.

"Yes," she said, "it's the Benz out there."

Even before she had gone out to see, she hadn't had much doubt. There was none now. Harvey had come in while Beecham was there and as soon as he heard Beecham's voice he had gone out again, softly, surreptitiously—and fast, because he thought it was about the check Beecham had come. If only the lawyer hadn't been there Harvey would know of Elfrida's terrible crash, and that he didn't need to keep on running. Damn Beecham. Damn, damn, *damn*. A wave of fury engulfed her.

Olivia's voice pierced it. "Dace," she demanded, "Dace, what is it, what's the matter? Your color—are you sick? Have you got a chill? Wait a minute and I'll get you a drink."

Dace could trust Olivia. After childhood they hadn't seen a great deal of each other until the last year or so, but Olivia was just the same, a little vague sometimes and wrapped up in her own affairs, but absolutely reliable. Greedily swallowing half the Sctoch on the rocks her cousin put into her hand, Dace explained. Harvey had been in the house a short time ago but when he found the lawyer was there he had taken to his heels.

Olivia was all eyes. She stared at Dace, frowning and puzzled. "But—why?"

"Because he can't stand the man and never could. He hates the very sight of him."

"Well then," Olivia said comfortably, pouring herself a drink and sitting down and stretching her long, beautiful legs toward the fire, "your troubles are over. If the mountain of a man I bumped into coming through the gate was your lawyer, and Harvey was out in the street, he must have seen Beecham go and he'll be in any moment."

Dace wasn't nearly so sure. Criticism of any sort, even a touch of it, was like a spur to a nervous colt; it sent Harvey off on the wrong foot in half a dozen different directions. The head of the class—he had to be in the right and admired and well thought of, he couldn't bear being put in the wrong about anything. If he thought she knew about the forged check, that Beecham had told her about it, he would be hating to face her. The natural thing

43

for him to do in such a situation would be to move off and keep away and be elsewhere until the first shock was over. She couldn't talk about the check to Olivia, couldn't bring herself to mention it. She simply said, "Harvey walked out a good twenty minutes before Beecham went and he mightn't have seen him go."

Olivia said sensibly, "Well, he won't expect the man to spend the night here," which was true. Dace got up and went to the phone and called Irene Branch, but Irene couldn't help. She hadn't been able to give Harvey Dace's message to ring her because he hadn't turned up. Back at the fire again a new and disturbing idea struck Dace.

The Benz was out there in the street ready and waiting. Harvey might drive off in it again into the blue; he had plenty of money in his wallet. The car ought to be put out of his reach. She didn't want to leave the house. It ended up by Olivia's taking Dace's set of keys and driving the Benz, not to their own garage where Harvey could get at it, but to another one farther south and to the east, near Twentieth Street and Second Avenue.

When Olivia came back the two of them had dinner alone in the little white and gold dining room on the floor below at a table set for three. Dace said, "Mr. Allert won't be in, Gertrude," and the maid said, "Yes, Madam," and cleared away the extra place. How much did the servants know or guess? Plenty probably. In the middle of dinner Gerald called. He was thunderstruck at the news about Elfrida. He had been out of the city all day or he would have rung earlier. Harvey not back yet, and in complete ignorance of Elfrida's accident and that she was dying; it put a different complexion on things. Harvey had to be located. Gerald said that if he had left the car outside the house a couple of hours earlier he couldn't be far afield. "I'll have a look around."

Gerald knew Harvey's haunts far better than she did, Dace thought: the Tolmans, people called Gateway, a Betty Fried something's studio somewhere in the Village, the Greymoor bar, Fondi's, various pubs. More than once when they were first married, when she used really to worry at Harvey's nonappearance when he should have been home, Gerald had dug him out for her.

44

Gerald said he'd keep in touch with her and she went back to the table. Olivia finished her pudding with a sigh of repletion, and they went upstairs for coffee. Shortly after that the influx began.

Harvey's other cousin, Scott Evans, arrived first, bearing a large bunch of yellow roses slightly the worse for wear; he always brought Dace yellow roses. Scott was the black sheep of the family, a tall man with the haggard, slightly puffy face of a drinker and kind eyes, hound's eyes, always a little bloodshot. His suit was shabby but meticulously pressed—the trouble with him was that he drank his wardrobe. In spite of his drinking and general improvidence Dace couldn't help liking him.

Scott knew about Elfrida; a friend of his had heard it from Joan Longstreet. He was incurious. "Harvey not here? I guess he has a lot to do." His tone was wistful. He thought he'd just stop to say—well, it was terrible about poor old Elfrida and all that, but now Harvey would be on easy street.

Scott was at least frank about it. He also had been at the house yesterday afternoon, but he hadn't seen Harvey, he hadn't come in. He had run into Hugh Clavering near the gate and Clavering had told him Dace wasn't home. "I had the roses for you. I hope they're all right. I kept them in the icebox."

Dace said they were lovely and Olivia got a vase and put them in water. Scott was still there when to Dace's horror the Longstreets came in. They should have phoned, she should have instructed Gertrude to say she wasn't in, but it was too late. What was she to tell Joan? How long could she keep up this deception about Harvey? Joan's attention was at first diverted. Scott and she were certainly not kissing cousins. Everything in Joan's smart, upright, well-ordered and conventional existence was outraged by Scott, by his friends, his general conduct and his drinking. Her greeting to him was frosty.

It didn't bother Scott any, he winked at her unabashed. "You're looking well, cousin Joan. . . ."

"I'm afraid I can't return the compliment."

"You didn't let me finish. You're getting fat."

It was a red rag to a bull, Joan had trouble keeping her

45

weight down. She drew in her breath, presented him with an icy stare and a shoulder and turned to Dace. Then it began.

"You did get in touch with Harvey, darling? He's here?"

Dace didn't answer directly. She said Harvey had gone out, that he had left the house before dinner and didn't say when he'd be back, which was certainly true.

Joan was disappointed. "Oh, dear, we did want to see him. . . . How did he take it? It must have been a terrible shock to him, poor boy, he was so fond of Elfrida. How does he feel? He's going to have a great deal of responsibility, a lot thrust at him all at once." She said Kermit would be glad to help. So would she. Anything they could do, anything at all . . . She jangled the twisted strands of a jade necklace, made play with an exaggerated cigarette holder and went on being particularly Joanish, busy, sweet, unselfish, eager and determined to be of use, ruthlessly determined. She couldn't leave the subject of Elfrida alone. She had called the hospital at half past eight and talked to the head surgeon, but there was no hope; in fact it was a miracle that Elfrida was still alive. The sooner the end came the better—hopelessly crippled—no one could wish that for her—and then Hugh's name.

Joan proceeded in her usual left-handed way. She said that Elfrida's death would be a blow to Hugh, all that money cut off, no longer at his disposal. He had certainly been assiduous in dancing attendance on Elfrida, almost as though he were a son—it really had been slightly ridiculous—but then, Hugh Clavering was a man who knew which side his bread was buttered on.

She was making her husband uncomfortable. Kermit kept shifting in his chair. He looked at Scott's drink as though he would like a stiff one himself, and lit a cigarette with a movement that had a touch of savagery in it. Snapping off the lighter, it flew from his fingers and fell to the floor. Kermit stooped to pick it up and the toe of his shoe sent it skittering under the flounce of Olivia's chair to the right of the fire. "Oh, stupid of me," he muttered. Olivia got out of his way and Kermit groped under the chair exploringly and came up with the lighter—and something else.

It was Harvey's wallet.

The wallet bulged. The thousand dollars was still in it.

Joan stared at it. "Oops," she said, "Harvey must have dropped it, and not noticed," and Dace said yes, as casually as she could. But she knew that wasn't what had happened. Harvey hadn't dropped the wallet accidentally, it had fallen out of his pocket during the scrimmage with Hugh Clavering here in this room yesterday afternoon and had been kicked under the chair unnoticed. What was Harvey doing for money? He couldn't get far without some. . . . Perhaps *that* was why he had gone up to the Branches, to try and borrow from Irene, and then changed his mind. . . . Actually the wallet was a stroke of luck, a blessing in disguise. If he had the thousand dollars now, driven by panic after finding Beecham in the house, he might be off in earnest. . . . She took the wallet from Kermit, crossed the floor and locked it safely in the desk.

Presently Scott finished his drink and said good night. Then Joan gave up the idea of seeing Harvey reluctantly, and she and Kermit went, sparked by a remark of Olivia's. She said bluntly out of a pause, "Dace, you're exhausted, your eyes are closing."

It was a relief to have the house empty, the maids had already gone; it was the only relief there was. Harvey didn't appear, he didn't put his key in the lock, the front door didn't open, but Dace told herself that it was early yet. She and Olivia talked desultorily about the wallet, how fortunate it was that Harvey didn't have much money, and settled down to wait. Olivia pored over a textbook—she was trying to teach herself stenography—and Dace tried to read. The type might have been so much Sanskrit. Lamplight and stillness, the sheen of brocade, the gleam of polished wood, Olivia's bent head, the purr of the fire—the outward order and serenity remained wearyingly, and maddeningly, unbroken.

Staring at the fire Dace saw pictures in the glowing core of it, a picture of Harvey in some bar downing drinks and determined to stay till the last minute, afraid to come home, afraid to face her. There were loads of places where he could get credit. She kept glancing at the clock. Half past ten, a quarter of eleven, exasperation added itself to her worry. Why was Harvey being so *stupid?* He would have to come home in the end. What good were these delaying tactics doing him? But he wouldn't think of that—put off the evil hour, something may happen. This time he was making a bad mistake. All he had to do to have his apprehensions, fears, stripped away was to walk in the front door.

At eleven Olivia went around to the delicatessen for cigarettes; they had both been smoking more heavily than usual. While she was gone the phone rang and Dace sped to it. It wasn't Harvey, it was Gerald Straws, and Gerald had drawn a blank. Harvey wasn't in any of his usual haunts but Gerald refused to worry. When Dace told him about the wallet, that Harvey had no money, he said, good, that maybe Harvey had put the tap on someone for a few dollars but that wouldn't last him long.

Gerald's detachment was in abeyance, he was kind. "That husband of yours is holed up somewhere having a whale of a time, he'll probably roll in at around four A.M. with a skinful. You know him. . . . Don't forget that he hasn't the slightest idea of what happened to Elfrida." He asked about Elfrida, and Dace said at last report early in the evening she was still alive but only just. Then Olivia came back with the cigarettes and settled down to her work again and Dace lit a fresh cigarette and wandered restlessly around the room.

Gerald was right. It wouldn't be the first time Harvey had closed the town up. And there was another thing, he had only the clothes he stood up in. That would make him unhappy—he was a cat for comfort. Also the car was out of his reach—which was one mercy.

Olivia took off her glasses and looked at Dace. "I know," she said sympathetically. "It's this waiting. But it really isn't late, not for a night owl like Harvey. You know what I think we ought to do? I think we ought to go to bed. What's the use of your sitting up stewing? That's not going to bring him home any sooner, and you'll be a wreck tomorrow. Leave the doors between your rooms open—you're a light sleeper—and you'll hear Harvey when he comes in."

"I don't think I'll be able to sleep," Dace objected.

"Then take a pill and leave a note on Harvey's bed about Elfrida and tell him to wake you." She got up with

48

decision. "Come on, Dace, let's shut up shop." Dace said all right wearily. They put the screen in front of the fire, checked the windows and drew the bolt on the back door. They left the front door unchained, and lights on in the living room and in the lower and upper halls.

By twelve o'clock they were both in bed, Olivia on the third floor, Dace on the second. The note about Elfrida was skewered to Harvey's pillow with a corsage pin. He couldn't overlook it. Dace's door, leading to the bath and intervening dressing room, was open; so was Harvey's at the other end of the short inner corridor. The light in his room—she had left the bed lamp on—was a pale blur on darkness. Dace tried to sleep without a pill, couldn't, and got up and took one. The last time she looked at the clock it said one-twenty. After that she drifted off.

She woke with a feeling of confinement, of being shut in, isolated. Her curtains were drawn and the room was completely black except for the illuminated clock face that said ten of three. It took her a few seconds to realize that the reason the room was so dark was that the inner door that led to Harvey's room was closed.

She sat up abruptly. Harvey was home. He had closed her door. Why hadn't he waked her? He must have seen the note about Elfrida. She threw the covers aside, got up and snatched at the robe across the foot of the bed. The air was cold. Pulling folds of yellow wool around her she went down the little corridor to Harvey's room.

She couldn't open his door. It was locked on the inside. "*Harvey*," she called, twisting the knob, "*Harvey*."

There was no answer and no sound of movement inside his room. She turned back, sped across her room and on into the outer hall. It was in darkness, too; the lights were out. She pressed a switch and ran down the hall and into Harvey's room by the door there; it wasn't locked. His bed lamp was off. She pressed the button. Light from the crystal chandelier in the ceiling fell on emptiness. But Harvey's overcoat was there, the dark blue vicuña coat he was so fond of and that he had worn when he left the house yesterday afternoon. It was lying across the bed, which was otherwise undisturbed. The amber satin spread was smooth, and the note—her eyes halted—was gone.

Harvey must be downstairs. Perhaps he was hungry and

he was getting himself something out of the refrigerator. She flew for the stairs, calling his name.

The lower hall and the living room were both in darkness. She kept putting on lights as she went. Olivia had heard her calling and joined her, tumbling down the stairs in her bare feet, struggling into a robe. "Harvey's back," Dace told her.

But Harvey wasn't. The two of them went through the entire house, looking into even the most unlikely places, even up in the attic, as a matter of form, because after the first minute or two it was obvious that except for themselves the house was empty. Harvey had come, and he had gone. The odd, the inexplicable thing about it, was that when he left he went by the back door. The bolt on it had been released, and was shoved back.

Both of them were bemused. "Maybe he left a note for you," Olivia suggested. "Maybe he didn't want to wake you. Maybe he's gone up to the hospital to see Elfrida."

But there was no note, on the mantel in the living room, the desk there, the desks upstairs, anywhere at all.

They looked in his room again. Harvey had changed his clothes. The gray flannel suit he had been wearing, the shirt, shoes, socks, everything, were thrown into the bottom of his wardrobe in an untidy heap. He had put on a heavy tweed suit, and his tan ulster, and packed a bag, the pigskin bag. Drawers were disturbed, tumbled. Also his hairbrushes, his toothbrush and one of his razors were gone. Dace's note about Elfrida was lying in the bottom of the trashbasket crumpled into a ball, but there was no message from him, no explanation whatever of why he had come and gone silently, secretly, without a word. . . .

Suddenly Dace thought of the wallet in the living-room desk, of the thousand dollars in it. Downstairs again, she hurried across the living room and raised the desk lid. The little satinwood drawer was pulled out. More emptiness, shining emptiness except for some coins. Both Harvey's wallet and the forty dollars in housekeeping cash were gone.

Standing there, looking into the empty drawer, instantly, and unjustly, the memory of Scott Evans flashed across Dace's mind—Scott, who was always hard up, staring at the stuffed wallet when Kermit Longstreet handed it to her earlier that night and she put it away in the desk. Scott had nothing to do with this. Harvey had a key to the desk drawer, a little brass key among the many on his key ring. Her key was in her purse. They sometimes locked up things they didn't want the maids to see. The drawer hadn't been broken open. A key had been used

. . . .

Dace was gazing at the forty-five cents in change that was all Harvey had left her, when a series of thundering raps smashed the night stillness. Someone was hammering on the front door.

FIVE

"You ladies all right? Anything wrong here? Anybody try to break in?"

Outlined against darkness patrolman Hardy was young, tall, thin, dark-haired and earnest. Olivia had pulled the door open to find him standing just outside. He stepped into the hall and closed the door behind him. It was bitterly cold. He looked from one girl to the other, taking in their robes and bare feet and their scared white faces.

It was Olivia who spoke. Dace was too stupified by what Harvey had done, his whole procedure, and by that terrible knocking, to get hold of her voice at once.

"No, Officer," Olivia told him, "we don't think so. We did think we heard a noise down here a little while ago, but when we came down there was no one and the doors and windows were all locked and nothing was disturbed."

Hardy then told them that about half an hour earlier he had seen a man come sneaking out of the court through the iron gate onto Thirty-seventh Street, a fellow in a kind of pale coat. He wouldn't have thought much about it if it hadn't been for the fact that the moment the man set eyes on him he had ducked back through the gate in a hurry. Hardy had entered the court and looked around thoroughly, but everything was dark and quiet and there was nobody in sight. Whoever the man was he could have gone over the back fences or into one of the two apartment houses that backed on the far side of the court. Anyhow there was no one there, so Hardy had resumed his beat. And then, passing the court on a return trip, he looked through the gate and had seen all the lights on in this house so he thought he better investigate.

Propped against the newel post because it was easier to lean against something than stand up straight, Dace understood it at once. "Fellow in a . . . pale coat"—the tan tweed ulster gone from upstairs. It was Harvey the policeman had seen leaving the court—and Harvey didn't want to be seen, stopped, interrogated. He had run back into the court, opened the front door with his keys and gone out through the rear door—you could make your way through a couple of gardens and along a narrow tunnel to Thirty-sixth Street that way. Harvey was evidently convinced that the police were after him, in spite of the fact that he now knew about Elfrida, and that she was dying. He must think she had started proceedings against him before she left New York on the day of her accident. That was why he had come and gone secretly, afraid to wake Dace, easing her bedroom door shut, afraid she'd argue with him, try to make him stay and face the music. It wasn't true that Elfrida had started anything but Dace decided that the less attention the house and their private affairs attracted, the better. . . . The first thing to do was to get rid of this policeman.

She and Olivia accompanied officer Hardy on the tour of the entire house he insisted on making. He didn't find anything because there was nothing to find—they had rebolted the back door earlier. Dace didn't want to show haste or strain, she was gracious. Wouldn't the officer like a drink or a cup of coffee or something before he left? Hardy said wistfully that at that he would like something to warm him up, the night would freeze your ears off and no fooling, but he'd better get back on the job, and went.

Locking the front door behind him and turning away from it, Dace wondered what Olivia was thinking. What could she think? Certainly Harvey's behavior was more than peculiar, without the clue of the check he had forged. The only thing to do was to tell Olivia the truth about the

53

check. She was naturally reticent, never talked idly and she could be as silent as the grave—she had known months before anyone else that Mary and Gil Marsden were married and had never revealed it by the flick of an eyelash—and besides that she had a lot of common sense.

Over coffee in front of the rebuilt fire—they were too wakeful to go back to bed—Dace brought out the whole painful story of Harvey and the check. After a first astonished exclamation Olivia listened in round-eyed silence. She was startled and surprised, but she didn't on the whole seem to be particularly shocked. Taking off her glasses and wiping them on a fold of her scarlet dressing gown and putting them on again, she shook her head.

"Oh, Dace, the *idiot* . . . And yet in a way you can't blame Harvey too much—Elfrida Allert's getting everything, or almost everything when his father died, and then charging him rent for this house . . . Harvey didn't stop to think. . . . I suppose in a way he looks on the money as his own—which it will be now, it was only his stepmother's for life—and you can't rob yourself."

As for Beecham, she said that even if Elfrida had told the lawyer—and there was no proof that she had—he would know where his best interest lay. Harvey would come into a lot of money and Beecham had always handled the Allert affairs, at a nice price. With Elfrida dead they would never hear a whisper of the check. The bank would be quietly told to lay off, and that everything was fine. She admonished Dace to stop worrying her head, torturing herself. When nothing happened Harvey would get over his jitters and come home. She added rather thinly, "But I must say I think Hugh Clavering had little to do to come here yesterday afternoon and tackle Harvey about what was absolutely none of his business—none whatever."

Looking into the fire over hands clasped in her lap Dace said that Hugh hadn't meant it that way, that he had simply wanted to help and Olivia shrugged. She was more concerned with Dace and Harvey and the situation as it was. When Harvey came in and found Beecham in the house that afternoon, he didn't know anything about Elfrida or her terrible accident, what had happened to her, and it was easy to see why he had jumped to the conclusion that the lawyer was there about the check. But now—well, he had to be found and told that everything was all right and that there was nothing to run away from. The only trouble was that while before he was practically penniless, he now had his wallet with the thousand dollars in it. The money made a lot of difference. Before he had been tied close to home; now he could go anywhere. She turned decisively in her chair. "Dace, Gerald Straws is Harvey's friend. He'll do anything for Harvey—and he's a man. I think you ought to tell Gerald Straws the whole business."

Dace agreed reluctantly. "I hate even Gerald to know—he's got a sort of priggish streak in him—but I suppose I ought to tell him. He'll stand a better chance of finding Harvey—and besides, Harvey will listen to Gerald when he won't to me or anybody else."

The tightness under her midriff began to go. She had been right to tell Olivia the truth. Her direct, uncomplicated response and her sturdy common sense were heartening. Also her lack of condemnation of Harvey. They talked a little longer and then, at shortly after five, they went upstairs. Olivia said she was going to get some sleep—it was her Saturday to work and she had to go to the office—and she advised Dace to get some rest herself.

In her bedroom with the curtains drawn back Dace settled herself on the chaise and watched the blackness of the winter night give way to the first gray of dawn over the leafless trees, their branches still outlined with snow. Day was easier than night, safer somehow; nothing was quite so terrible when it was light. She closed her eyes for just a minute. She woke at almost eleven to pale sunlight filling the room. It was the phone that woke her. Harvey . . . She banged her knee getting to it, snatched up the instrument. Gertrude was answering from downstairs. A man's voice said, "Yes, Mrs. Allert, please." Dace recognized his voice at once. It was Hugh Clavering. She said, "I'll take it, Gertrude," and Gertrude got off the wire.

Hugh hadn't asked for Harvey. After what had happened between them on Thursday afternoon it was understandable. Instead he said almost exactly what he had said when she had encountered him in the falling snow near the entrance to the court two days ago. "Dace, I've got to see you. I don't want to come there. . . . Could you meet me?"

Again he was grave, curt, unlike himself. Harvey, Dace thought tightening, something's happened to Harvey. . . . No, it couldn't be that or Hugh wouldn't have said he didn't want to come to the house. She got her breath.

"Is it important, Hugh?"

"It's very important."

There was no reason why she shouldn't meet Hugh Clavering as far as the world in general was concerned, Joan Longstreet's coy and suggestive glances the other day notwithstanding. Less than half an hour later Dace was seated opposite him at a table in the dining room of the small hotel on Fiftieth Street where he was staying. Hugh was in the middle of breakfast. He looked tired. He said he had been at the hospital up in Putnam the night before and had slept late. Dace asked about Elfrida and he said she was still alive—the doctors marveled at it, but she had a good deal of strength. It couldn't possibly last much longer. He hoped not, her injuries were frightful. Mercifully she felt nothing, she was in deep coma. He insisted on ordering coffee for Dace. After it came and the waiter went, she said, "What is it, Hugh? Why did you ask me to meet you?"

For a man who knew his own mind and never under any circumstance hesitated to speak it, he took a long time to answer. His eyes explored her face, moved off, came back again. Hugh wouldn't look like this for nothing. . . . The fear Dace had felt the evening before with Beecham came flooding, great waves of it. . . . It was worse this time. It inundated her. She got her head above water.

"Please, Hugh," she said sharply, "*please.*"

"Yes." He nodded and told her.

Harvey had been right to be afraid, and she and Olivia had been wrong. . . . There was a warrant out for Harvey's arrest.

A waiter in a jacket that didn't quite fit flicked a distant table with a napkin. A woman with a green bird in her hat crunched toast loudly. Beyond the archway into the bar ice was being shaken. Dace raised her coffee cup to her lips and put the cup down. The spoon on the saucer

56

tinkled. Then sound was wiped out, and sight, and the room and everything in it vanished. She was seeing Harvey seized and arrested, in prison, behind bars; seeing the headlines in the papers, Harvey branded in letters a foot high as a thief, a forger. . . . The publicity, the disgrace of it would kill him. . . . He couldn't possibly survive. . . . She was on her feet, and then Hugh's hand was on her arm and she was sitting down again and the room was settling into place.

Hugh said, "Don't take it so hard, Dace."

His voice was gentle. She couldn't stand the solicitude in it, the sympathy in his eyes. She sat up straighter and reached for a cigarette.

"I won't. . . . I'm being a fool. It's just the—the shock."

"I know, but I had to tell you."

She wished he'd be quiet, that he wasn't there; nothing mattered now but Harvey. She said of course, and Hugh went on with it. After he left Elfrida last Thursday afternoon and before she herself left New York, Elfrida had talked to Beecham on the phone. It was then that she had told him about Harvey and the check.

Hugh said, cold anger in him, "This is Beecham's work, not Elfrida's. If she hadn't had that dreadful accident, if you had been able to get in touch with her, the whole business, all of it, would have blown over and she would have changed her mind. I know she would. I'm as sure of it as I am of sitting here—but that's water over the dam." He hesitated and went on, "When you spoke to Harvey about the check . . ."

"I didn't speak to him."

"You didn't?"

"I couldn't." Dace was ice-cold now. She outlined succinctly what had happened: Harvey's absence when she got home Thursday afternoon, his staying out all that night, his riding around all yesterday in the car, his finding Beecham in the house when he came back late yesterday afternoon, his retreat, his return last night to change his clothes and pack a bag and get his wallet with the thousand dollars in it and his flight out the back way from the policeman.

Hugh listened attentively in frowning silence. When she finished he said thoughtfully, "It's unfortunate that he managed to get hold of his wallet, now that he has plenty of money it's going to be harder to locate him—but in the meantime Beecham's got to be stopped before he goes any further. Just because there's a warrant out for Harvey's arrest doesn't necessarily mean that this thing need ever come to trial, or even that it has to be brought out in the open at all. It's true that Beecham is one of Elfrida's executors, but I'm the other, and I'll have something to say. When Beecham called me this morning I didn't have time to go into that angle, I wanted to get hold of you right away. Now . . ."

He said that flight was no good, in fact it was worse than nothing, and that the sooner Harvey put himself back in circulation and into the hands of a good lawyer, the better. Dace suggested Harvey's cousin, Kermit Longstreet, but Hugh said no, it would have to be a criminal lawyer. He watched her flinch, put a hand over hers hard and briefly, and went on reassuring, comforting her. Everything was going to be all right. Beecham was an ass. The estate would be Harvey's—and money talked. He'd have a look around for Harvey himself. He asked questions, names of friends, places where he might take refuge, places they had gone together, scribbling on the back of an envelope. He'd also, if she wanted, consult someone about the best counsel Harvey could get, someone tiptop, and in addition he'd have it out with Beecham.

At the end of another five minutes he signaled the waiter and paid the check. He told her that the thing for her to do now was to go home and wait. Harvey might get tired of running and come back of his own accord. Outside the hotel under the canopy he studied her face. "Good girl," he said softly, ran a finger down her cheek, hailed a cab, put her into it and closed the door.

The drive was a short one. Short as it was, Dace was almost cheerful when she got out at the corner of Park, and walked down over pavements slick with icy snow, through the gate and into the court. The cold air and the thin sunlight were like wine, strengthening, heady. She felt light and buoyant, and at the same time vaguely guilty. She rebuked herself for the guilty feeling. It was stupid.

58

No one could help being encouraged by Hugh's calm strength and his decisiveness. If it was for her sake, well, all this would soon be over and they wouldn't be seeing each other any more. . . . Harvey needed help and Hugh was going to give it to him, better than his friends could, and that was what mattered. For one thing Beecham would listen to Hugh where he would brush her or Gerald Straws aside as prejudiced. She mounted the short flight of steps and used her key.

When she went in Gertrude was hovering in dimness at the rear of the hall. She came walking quickly toward Dace. Her eyes were big with excitement under a cap a little askew on her frizzled head as she said that there were two men to see Madam. She'd put them in the living room. She hoped she'd done right. . . . They were from the police.

"Oh? Really? Thank you, Gertrude."

Dace stripped off her gloves coolly and tossed them down on the table under the mirror. She had expected some development, another visit from Beecham perhaps and a formal notification from him of Harvey's impending arrest; she hadn't expected anything like this so soon, without the slightest warning. She stifled a rush of interior panic. If it hadn't been for Hugh she would have been overcome. . . . One of the things she had determined to do in the cab was to straighten Harvey's room and remove all traces of his having been in it last night.

That living-room door was closed. There was still time to do that. She nodded a dismissal to Gertrude and started for the stairs. It was scarcely likely that the police would want to examine Harvey's bedroom but it was a possibility. Before she was level with the living-room door it opened.

A tall man, very tall—he was well over six feet—looked out at her. Thick, dark hair touched with gray; deep-set, dark eyes in a long, intelligent face; she had seen this man before, on several occasions, somewhere in a crowd, at the theater or in one or another of the night clubs. He was a man you noticed, remembered.

He said interrogatively, "Mrs. Allert?"

His voice was pleasant, his manner courteous, easy. There was no threat whatever in him. He introduced himself.

"Inspector McKee, Mrs. Allert. If we could have a few minutes of your time?"

"Oh?" Looking up at him Dace raised her brows, showing surprise but not too much of it, and thanked God again that Hugh had warned her. "Of course, Inspector."

She gave her things to Gertrude, who had continued to hover—get rid of this girl, she thought, Gertrude was far too curious—and went through the door the Inspector held open, and on into the living room. He closed the door behind her and introduced a second man standing near the desk between the windows—a smallish, sandy-haired individual with a little tan mustache, who looked rather like a racing tout. His brown suit was too tight for him.

"This is Mr. Cairn from the district attorney's office."

Dace showed a little more surprise. "Mr. Cairn."

"Mrs. Allert."

It was like a ballet. She bowed and the sandy-haired Cairn bowed, and they all sat down.

McKee had been studying Dace. Looks, brains and guts, he decided. A fighter. Nervous—but that was natural enough. The delicately-boned, pointed face, wide at the cheekbones and narrow at the chin, had something more than mere beauty. It aroused your interest and held it with the play of expression. The gray eyes under the broad brow were steady, unclouded; Mrs. Allert had a good grip on herself. McKee didn't like the errand he was saddled with because the district attorney, John Francis Dwyer, had been got at by Charlie Beecham. He himself wouldn't have paid any attention to Dwyer, but Dwyer had been with Commissioner Carey, and Carey had asked the Scotsman to come here and have a look as a personal favor. "I don't know whether there's anything to it or not, McKee—it may be a mare's-nest and in any case it wouldn't be in your hands—but I'd like to have your opinion."

Tackle the obvious angle first, McKee thought, and went into it directly. This girl would appreciate that; she looked like a direct person herself. He said that the district attorney's office wanted to talk to Mr. Harvey Allert. He wasn't at his office, they had checked before coming here to the house. "Your maid says Mr. Allert isn't in. Can you tell us where we can locate him?"

Dace settled back and made herself easy, crossing one knee over the other and lighting a cigarette she didn't want. Volunteer nothing. Speak when you were spoken to and answer only the questions you were asked. She combined a faint look of trouble with a rueful amusement at McKee's question.

"Where Harvey can be located—I'm afraid I can't tell you that, Inspector."

Both men stared, and she went on calmly "I know it sounds stupid but it happens to be true." A faint flush at having to explain intimacies to men who were strangers to her tinged her pale cheeks. "Thursday afternoon, this last Thursday afternoon, my husband and I had a quarrel. It was—rather a violent one and Harvey got very angry at me and he—well, he walked out and I haven't seen him since."

Cairn turned and looked sharply at McKee. McKee looked at Dace.

"You mean Mr. Allert has left you?"

"Oh, no," she exclaimed, smiling, "nothing like that. But when Harvey gets into a rage, or upset, it's what he always does. It doesn't really mean anything. He'll stay away for a while until he calms down and then he'll come back as though nothing had ever happened and everything will be all right. It's always like that." She shrugged lightly.

Was Mercedes Allert being a little too ingenuous—the amused wife explaining a husband's peccadilloes with acceptance and tolerant resignation? McKee showed his gravity. "Mrs. Allert, I'm afraid we have bad news for you."

In spite of the fact that she had been warned and knew what was coming, it was still a shock when it came officially, in actual words.

The charge against Harvey was forging and uttering.

It hit her hard and she showed it, sitting very still, her faint color fading, her expressive eyes darkening with pain. They gave her time and then Cairn went into the details, the cashing of the check for a thousand dollars drawn on Elfrida Allert's account and bearing her signature, the bank officer's suspicion, the contacting of Mrs. Allert Senior, and her statement that she had sent Harvey Allert no such check.

Dace listened in silence, trying to recover herself and saying nothing except, flatly—and having trouble speaking at all in those first few moments—that she didn't believe that her husband had done what they said he did. Harvey wasn't here and so they couldn't serve him with any warrant; she didn't know much but she did know that. She waited for the two men to get up and go. They didn't go. Mr. Cairn finished and then the Inspector took over.

He began innocuously. First he wanted to know what the quarrel between Dace and Harvey last Thursday afternoon had been about. She frowned, thought back or pretended to, and gave it up with a shrug. Nothing and everything, she said; she simply couldn't recall what had started it. It was just one of those things. McKee then began asking her questions about Harvey and Elfrida and Elfrida's car, the Torshe-Hamton.

Dace answered him truthfully. Yes, Elfrida had asked Harvey to check on the Torshe and see if everything was all right, and he had taken it for a run through the park on Wednesday afternoon. He was excellent with cars, better than most mechanics. He said all the car needed was a little tuning up, and tightening here and there. He did that out in the court, then put the Torshe in the Stamford Garage Wednesday night. The next morning, Thursday, on his way to work he dropped the car off at the Plaza and left it for Elfrida with the doorman.

Watching Dace closely McKee saw that she had no slightest idea where his questions were leading. But she was beginning to be puzzled, and her puzzlement grew. All at once she stopped talking and looked at him frowningly.

"But—I don't think I understand. . . . Why are you asking me all this, Inspector?"

As far as McKee could see, take it by and large, it wasn't much of a case, Beecham to the contrary. In any event, now that this girl had made a statement she was entitled to a warning. He gave it to her.

Harvey Allert was suspected of having brought about Elfrida's accident by tampering with her car. If this was so and if she died—when she died—her death would be murder.

SIX

Dace sat staring at the tall Scotsman as though he were a piece of the wall, her eyes brilliant. Murder . . . Harvey a murderer . . . The concept was so completely ridiculous that her first impulse was to smile. He had a violent temper, granted—she thought fleetingly of some of his explosions; his throwing Dona Blair's pom through a window last year—a ground-floor window luckily—when it nipped him; of his smashing things recklessly when he was in a rage, like the Chinese ginger jar on last Thursday afternoon. Concede all these things—this charge was different. This was a charge of sly, calculated, cold-blooded murder, implemented in advance, carefully planned—and Harvey didn't plan. He was a creature of impulse, often chopping and changing in mid flight.

McKee had been prepared for attack, for hysterics, tears, violent denial, outrage. All Dace said after a long reflective pause was, "Why do the police suspect Harvey of such a—a frightful thing, on what grounds?"

The Scotsman gave her Beecham's reasoning. There was the forged check for instance. According to Beecham, Harvey had never expected the check to be challenged; he had figured on his stepmother's being dead before any question as to its validity came up. Beecham termed the tuning up of the car opportunity, and as for motive, Harvey Allert needed money badly. Elfrida was the obstacle to his getting his hands on a lot of it, so he had removed her. According to McKee's thinking, Charlie Beecham had one thing and one thing only with which to bolster his extremely sketchy case. Perhaps it was so, perhaps it wasn't; see what this girl had to say. "Mrs. Allert, at what time after your quarrel with him on last Thursday afternoon did your husband leave this house?"

Dace lifted her hands and let them fall. She said she didn't know. She explained about leaving Harvey in possession of the field and going out for a walk herself, about Harvey's having let her cousin Olivia Wood in at around half past four, about Olivia's going out again to post letters, and about Harvey's being gone when she herself got back to the house at shortly before six o'clock.

"So you can't say whether your husband was or was not in the house at around a quarter of five on last Thursday afternoon?" Dace couldn't and McKee said, "I see," absently.

One of the state troopers on the scene of Elfrida Allert's accident had gone to the hospital with the injured woman in the ambulance in case she should recover consciousness. She hadn't recovered consciousness, but she had muttered brokenly at one point. What she said was, "Harvey . . . Harvey Allert . . . New York . . ." and then sank back into the depths again. Long before the hospital had been able to contact the farm in Duchess County, to which Mrs. Allert had been proceeding when she crashed, the state policeman acted. Figuring that Harvey Allert was the one to be notified—same name—he got the number from information and called this house and, assertedly, talked to Harvey Allert.

If Mrs. Allert had said her husband was not in the house when the trooper called at four-fifty P.M., that Allert had already gone out, and could have proved that he wasn't there and so consequently couldn't have been the man the state trooper talked to, it would have knocked the props from under Beecham. Such not being the case, Allert's behavior after having been informed of his stepmother's fatal accident did look remarkably like flight; a determination to lie low and keep out of the way until he

65

saw how the wind blew, whether any suspicion had been aroused, whether, if Elfrida knew anything significant, leading, she spoke, or died without speaking.

McKee told Dace about the telephone call from the state policeman at four-fifty Thursday afternoon and she fought him, calmly. She said that it mightn't have been Harvey who answered the phone that afternoon, he might have been gone by then. "It could have been someone else, Inspector." She explained Olivia's leaving the door on the latch when she went to post her letters, and Kermit Longstreet's coming later and finding the door unlocked and the house empty.

"Can you think of any good reason why anyone else should have answered the phone and taken that call—and then walked out as though the message was of no importance, Mr. Allert?"

Dace couldn't, she didn't attempt to, she simply shook her head after a pause for reflection, but she refused to give ground, protecting her husband every inch of the way. Why not? McKee thought. She was Harvey Allert's wife and there was a great deal of money involved. When Elfrida died Harvey would sweep the board—if he was innocent—a man couldn't benefit as the result of a crime. The Scotsman settled down to work.

It was Dace's first experience of the monotony, and the deadliness, of a police investigation, particularly where homicide was concerned. She was exhausted before it was over, for then. In the main she was truthful. She didn't mention the fisticuffs between Hugh Clavering and Harvey when Hugh came on Thursday afternoon because it had no bearing; she would have liked to keep Hugh's name out of it altogether but she couldn't. When McKee asked her what she had done while she was out of the house after the quarrel with her husband, whether she had simply wandered around in the snow for more than two hours, her hand was forced. Joan Longstreet had seen her with Hugh. . . .

She said that when she was almost home she had run into Hugh Clavering, a connection of Elfrida Allert's by marriage, and had had a drink with him in the Rockingham around the corner. She told the Inspector about Harvey's call to the Branches in Hastings yesterday, about his driving back to New York yesterday afternoon and parking their car outside the gate, of his return to the house late last night or rather early this morning, for a change of clothes and to get money, and of his taking off again before she had a chance to talk to him—all of which the police could get from others.

McKee said, "He left without a word to you—how did you know he had come and gone?"

She said stiffly, "From the condition of his room later." She refused to concede Harvey's forging of the check in so many words. That would be stupid. Hugh Clavering was going to try and stop Beecham from further action, but let the police think what they wanted to about that. It couldn't be helped. His fear about what might happen to him because of his forging was the only possible explanation of the way he was acting, and in the face of this new and graver, this terrible charge about Elfrida and her car, the check was almost insignificant.

When McKee had milked her dry of all the evidence she intended to contribute he and Cairn went upstairs and looked over Harvey Allert's bedroom, where the forging of the check had probably been done; it wasn't work a man would carry on in an office or in a living room. Cairn appropriated various items, some specimens of Allert's handwriting, a handsome gold and onyx pen on a stand and another smaller pen in a drawer.

When they took their departure a few minutes later McKee had in his possession several small snapshots, poor, of Harvey Allert and a description of the clothes Allert was currently wearing and the bag he was carrying. Mercedes Allert remained cool and ungiving to the last. "Of course I don't mind your taking those pictures, Inspector, certainly not. I want my husband back just as much—more—than you do so that he can dispose of this—wicked nonsense about Elfrida's car."

Outside, with the door closed behind them, descending the small flight of steps in wintry sunlight, Cairn said explosively, "Well." It wasn't a question. McKee nodded. He knew what Cairn meant. If the story Mrs. Allert had told them was true Harvey Allert's behavior was an open confession of guilt as far as the forged check was concerned; he was definitely on the run. Elfrida Allert's car was something else again.

The custom-built Torshe-Hamton was being thoroughly gone over by men who knew their business, but there was no verdict yet. Also Elfrida herself was still alive and it was just possible that she might speak before she died, and that if she did she might have something important to say. The thing to do was to bag Allert quietly and without fanfare and wait and see what turned up. Meanwhile check on the general background and the tale Mrs. Allert had told them. The list of the people to be interviewed was short. Might as well get it over with now, he decided, before they could make any little arrangements among themselves. He began with Mrs. Allert's cousin, Olivia Wood.

"Oh no, Inspector—*no*." Olivia Wood sat stiffly erect in the chair behind the desk in the little cubicle at Batsons' Research where she worked and where McKee found her. She was on the large side, a very pretty girl with a skin like a peach, big, solemn brown eyes behind glasses and an excellent figure—a demure Juno in tailored clothes. Her tempo was slower than her cousin's, there was nothing wistful in her, no flash or dazzle. She was serious, literal, and with her feet on the ground. She knew about the check Harvey Allert had allegedly forged, she didn't know about the warrant for his arrest; therefore, Mrs. Allert hadn't yet got in touch with her. She was horrified.

She corroborated every detail of Mercedes Allert's story, with one important change and several small ones. Mrs. Allert hadn't mentioned the knock-down-drag-out fight between her husband and Hugh Clavering on last Thursday afternoon. Miss Wood said that Harvey had admitted her to the house at around half past four and she had gone upstairs to dry her hair and fix her face. When she came down the two men were at it hammer and tongs in the living room. It only lasted a minute. Then Hugh Clavering went, after asking curtly where Dace was, and Harvey picked himself up off the floor and went upstairs. He wasn't hurt except for a cut lip he kept patting with a handkerchief, but he was pretty furious. She herself had had no idea what had provoked the fight until her cousin told her about the check.

68

She said, "I suppose Elfrida Allert sent Hugh Clavering to the house, but you can hardly blame Harvey for losing his temper. It's a pretty terrible thing to be accused of, particularly when you're innocent."

Her defense of Allert was calm and forceful. She covered the Thursday afternoon and evening and the following day and night. When she got back from posting some letters Dace was there but Harvey was gone. She described Harvey's return while the lawyer was with Dace yesterday afternoon, his coming back in the middle of the night and leaving by the kitchen door on account of the policeman. McKee said, "Oh?" and she described what had happened, adding that Harvey didn't intend to be railroaded into jail by that horrid Beecham, that was why he had gone out the back door.

She had nothing more to contribute and McKee was about to leave her when the phone on her desk rang. She picked it up. Mercedes Allert was on the wire. Olivia Wood said, "Yes, Dace . . ." and listened. As she listened her half-averted face flushed rose-red up to the hairline and she said hastily, "Inspector McKee's here with me now—I'll call you back later," and hung up. She was flustered and ill at ease. She said nothing, wisely. Neither did McKee, but as he left the office he wondered idly why Mercedes Allert didn't want the police to know about the fight between her husband and Hugh Clavering on Thursday afternoon. Later on he got an answer of sorts from Charlie Beecham.

Before that the Allerts' maid, Gertrude Sims, verified Olivia Wood's account of what had taken place between Clavering and Allert. She hadn't actually seen the fight, but she had heard the uproar. She had returned to the house by way of the back door to get a parcel she had forgotten and she was in the room directly below the living room when the rumpus started. A heavy thud shook the ceiling and there was a terrific clatter. She had gone upstairs. When she reached the hall a man was just letting himself out through the front door and Miss Wood came out of the living room where she was talking to Mr. Allert and said everything was all right, so the maid had gone home.

When McKee went downtown at around five o'clock to

make his report Charlie Beecham was with the Commissioner. Beecham told the Scotsman about Dace and Hugh Clavering, that they had gone around together three or four years ago and all their friends had expected them to marry, but they hadn't. The lawyer said, "Naturally I looked into Clavering when he married Elfrida's niece, poor Dolly, later on. Nothing against him. Good at his work, industrial designing, although not much money in his end. Nice fellow and all that and Elfrida thought the world of him, but . . ." At the moment Beecham was out of temper with Hugh Clavering. Clavering treated forgery as though it were some sort of parlor game, thought they ought to lay off Harvey about the check. "I'll be damned if I do."

To the Commissioner, McKee gave it as his considered opinion that at the moment there was no solid ground for a charge of attempted murder against Harvey Allert. If Elfrida Allert's car had been tampered with, in all probability the traces of such tampering would have been obliterated in her crackup—the car was an almost complete wreck.

Beecham was a bulldog. He clung doggedly to his opinion. "You're wrong, McKee—dead wrong." He said Harvey Allert was an ill-conditioned, self-willed pup, and hated his stepmother, who had never done anything but good to him. Naturally she worried about the way he lived, his lack of seriousness, the way he threw up a job when he didn't like it, and above all his reckless extravangance troubled her—that was why she had decided to charge him rent for the Murray Hill house. She had wanted him to realize his responsibilities, come to his senses, where money was concerned. Instead, he had decided to kill her.

McKee was equally firm. Unless new evidence came up—and he didn't see where it was to come from—he said there was nothing on which they could act.

"You don't consider his running away, his taking it on the lam like this, anything, McKee?"

"The check, Counselor."

Beecham damned the check. Harvey had brass enough for anything. He knew his stepmother had been fatally injured, he had taken the phone call from the state trooper, and he was hiding out until she died for fear that in the meantime she might recover sufficiently to say something that would establish his guilt. Beecham was by turns angry, outraged, sarcastic—and finally he took on the role of prophet.

His last words as he got angrily to his feet and left the big, handsome office on the second floor of the long gray building on Centre Street were: "All right, Inspector, play it your way if you want to, but I'm warning you, here and now. You'll find out you're wrong. Wait and see."

The Scotsman didn't at all like Charlie Beecham's parting shot; Beecham knew Elfrida's stepson, and he didn't. Play along within reason, he thought as he went back uptown. Half an hour later a five-state alarm was out for Harvey Allert. There were no particulars and there was no definite charge. Allert was to be detained for questioning, if and when located, that was all. McKee wasn't hopeful of any immediate result. Allert's description, physique and clothes, brown hair, blue eyes, height, weight, wearing a light tan overcoat, etc., etc., would fit any number of men. Moreover, Allert could be thousands of miles away by now, he had plenty of money in his pocket. Men were sent backtracking on him in the hope of a lead to his whereabouts, and McKee turned his attention to other business.

SEVEN

Meanwhile for Dace, cooped up in the little house in the court on Murray Hill, the day had been long and wearing and the evening that followed on its heels was worse. She didn't dare go out. Harvey would hardly attempt to return to the house in broad daylight but he might telephone, unless he was afraid the phone would be tapped—which was not unlikely—considering the state he was in. And it might be at that, for all she knew. After the going over she had had from the Inspector, she was prepared for almost anything. Hugh and Gerald Straws both called her. Neither had had any success in locating Harvey or finding the slightest trace of him. Olivia had also called after Inspector McKee left her office.

Dace had no sooner asked her cousin not to mention the battle between Harvey and Hugh the other day than she regretted it. There was nothing to hide. It was just that she kept remembering Joan Longstreet's glance at Hugh in the Rockingham bar, the unspoken innuendo in her lightly raised brows and small smile. It was stupid to let it bother her. She didn't care a snap of her fingers for Joan and her opinions, which would naturally be of the worst, but there was Harvey to consider. She had never told Harvey about herself and Hugh, that they'd once been in love with each other. If Joan wanted to make any trouble, no doubt she could, but it was all water over the dam, and Harvey's anger and possible jealousy were trivialities in the face of what he was up against.

A warrant out for his arrest—she couldn't make herself at home with the thought. Each time she repeated it to herself it came as a fresh shock. As for that other allegation about Harvey and Elfrida's car, it was too absurd for serious consideration. Nevertheless it remained at the back of her mind as a shadow and as a goad, another reason why Harvey must come home, so that he could dispose of it effectually, once and for all.

Gerald Straws turned up at around five o'clock. She had told him that morning about Harvey and the check and what had happened during the night. Walking into the living room he said, "Nothing? No word?" and Dace shook her head. Gerald looked at her and swore softly. He was really disturbed. His face was tight and his lips compressed. "The damn fool . . . I'd like to beat him to a jelly." He asked her about the police, the men who had been there, who they were, and when Dace said a Mr. Cairn from the district attorney's office and an Inspector McKee, Gerald stopped lighting his pipe and stared at her fixedly.

"McKee . . . ? I know McKee—at least I know of him. He's a big wheel in Homicide. . . . What the devil was *he* doing here?"

Dace told him and Gerald started as though he had been shot.

"*What* . . . ? Elfrida's car . . . *Harvey* . . . Well I'll be damned."

Gerald seldom showed much strong emotion. He did then. Incredulousness was followed by cold fury. He said, his light eyes bright and still and oddly luminous, that Beecham must be out of his head, off the beam, around the bend. The idea was so palpably ridiculous that it wasn't even worth bothering about.

Gerald was Harvey's friend and he knew Harvey inside out. Sure as Dace was herself, Gerald's complete certainty was a comfort. "I wouldn't," he advised her, "say anything about this to anyone else if I were you." Olivia came in from work a few minutes later and Gerald knocked the dottle out of his pipe—the inevitable pipe

73

that so often served him as a substitute for a comment, an expected observation, or gave him time for a considered answer, so that he was seldom taken by surprise. Shortly after he went the Longstreets arrived.

They had come for a conference. They knew about the check; a detective had been with Kermit, asking questions about his visit to the house last Thursday afternoon. They were both grave, serious and indignant. Neither of them believed, so they said, that Harvey had forged any check. He had told Elfrida that the check had come in the mail so that was what had happened. Joan was the firmer and the more vociferous and forceful of the two. Either Elfrida had sent Harvey the check and then tried to get out of it for some reason or other—there was no denying that in ways she was queer; look at her sudden demand for the rent for this house, for instance—or if the check was a forgery then someone else had forged it, someone who had deliberately tried to blacken Harvey's name, someone who hated him.

When she said this, twisting the long string of beads around her neck, Joan looked at Dace meditatively, sleek and well-groomed and without a hair out of place. Her eyes were as blue and as hard as the huge blue dinner ring she wore.

Dace looked back at her evenly. "Are you referring to anyone in particular, Joan?"

But Joan refused open battle. Instead she attacked obliquely. She could understand Harvey's absence. He was upset and on edge, poor sweet, he wanted to get away by himself and think things out in solitude, lick his wounds alone somewhere—he'd always been like that. No doubt he had plenty to worry him . . . What he needed was sympathy and kindness and love. . . . Suddenly her eyes filled with tears. "I only hope he won't—won't do something terrible. . . . How do we know? How can we tell? He's been gone since last night, and not a word from him since then."

For once she seemed to be genuine and not putting on an act. Kermit got up and went over to her and scolded her gently. "Joan, stop it. Don't be such a fool—getting yourself all wrought up over nothing. Chimeras, bugaboos, creations of your own mind . . . Ridiculous. What you

74

need is a drink——one would do us all good."

"Maybe, just maybe . . ." Joan pressed quivering lips together and mopped tears from her make-up, Olivia went to get drinks, and Dace sat gazing into the fire. Suicide . . . That was what Joan meant. . . . Such a thought had never entered her head until then. . . . When Harvey was in one of his black moods his reason *was* temporarily obliterated——and it *was* a long time not to have heard from him. . . . Yesterday had been different. She had been able to follow his movements yesterday and understand them, but since three o'clock that morning there had been nothing at all. . . .

The horror Joan had conjured up had no basis in fact. Harvey was alive and well. Hugh called Dace while Kermit and Olivia were fixing highballs. Elfrida was sinking rapidly; he had just been talking to the head surgeon, a Dr. Alvarez. And Alvarez had also told him that earlier in the day Harvey had been on the phone to him. He had inquired at length as to his stepmother's condition, whether she had recovered consciousness or was likely to, and then he had announced his intention of going to the hospital that night. Hugh was going up himself and said, "When I find out what's what I'll phone you from there."

After hanging up and returning to the living room, Dace told the others about Harvey's telephone call to the hospital earlier that day. Joan threw herself back in her chair with a long sigh and closed her eyes for a moment. "Thank heavens," she exclaimed, "oh, thank heavens, Harvey's safe." Watching her go limp with relief Dace reflected that the one genuine thing about Joan was her feeling for Harvey. There was no pretense about it, she was deeply fond of him. Kermit was also very much relieved. His long, pleasant face cleared and he turned to Dace. "I didn't," he said, "want to mention this before, I didn't want to bother you, but as a matter of fact I want to see Harvey as soon as possible because . . ."

Dace listened to what Kermit went on to say in his rather hesitant voice in stunned silence. Harvey had borrowed three thousand dollars from Kermit Longstreet more than two months ago, promising to let him have it back in a few days. The loan hadn't been repaid, not a penny of it, and Kermit needed it for an insurance premium that was coming due. That was what he had stopped in to see Harvey about last Thursday afternoon.

Dace was appalled. Harvey had deceived her beautifully. He had been lying to her all along, pretending to economize, to make do with the money available, while all the time he had been spending borrowed money and going deeper into debt. . . . Where had the three thousand he had had from Kermit gone? She hadn't seen any of it—and how did he think he could possibly repay the three thousand? Now, yes, when Elfrida died, but he couldn't have known what was going to happen to her when he borrowed the money. . . . And yet it was typical of his happy-go-lucky approach, and his incurable and dangerous optimism, that could carry him to the lip of a precipice. Don't worry. Tomorrow will take care of itself. Everything's going to be all right. Something will turn up.

Another thought struck her, chillingly, and she shrank in her chair, her hands tightening on the arms. According to Beecham, Harvey had never expected the check for a thousand dollars to be challenged because Elfrida would be dead. Dace's own belief in his complete innocence as far as Elfrida's accident was concerned was unshaken, but Beecham wouldn't see it that way if he were to hear about this. . . .

Kermit went on talking, in his soothing, pleasant way. He wasn't really worried about his money—that would settle itself—but Harvey needed someone to advise him, tell him what to say and do, and what not to say in this matter of the check. Kermit proposed to drive up to the hospital at once—it would only take a little over an hour. He would wait there for Harvey to arrive and after Harvey had seen Elfrida he'd bring him back here to the house. Dace had better stay where she was—there was no use alerting the police, they might be watching her—until they had figured out a plan of approach, how best to handle things.

"All right with you, Dace?" Kermit asked and Dace nodded. It sounded sensible. She couldn't accomplish anything by going up there. Joan promptly announced her intention of driving up with Kermit, which was all to the good. Anything was preferable to her staying on in the house.

Kermit finished his drink briskly, saying that the sooner they got started, the better. Joan took out her compact. Again that flickering tongue of malice. Powdering her face she said, "I didn't know you were keeping in such close touch with Hugh Clavering, Dace. . . . Oh, well"—she gave her crisp little laugh and got up and into her coat— "in this case it was lucky, wasn't it?"

"My, my," Olivia said with her slow grin when the door closed behind the Longstreets, "and how did you like that? Joan Longstreet certainly has her knife out for you, Dace." She linked her hands behind her head and stretched out comfortably. "You know what I think? I think that woman would be delighted to see you and Harvey bust up, tickled pink—and that she means to lend a helping hand, if she can. And for why? Because Harvey, and Harvey's money, would come back into the family unencumbered. What she'd like to do would be to pick some nice girl for him she could twist around her finger. I'm sure that's what's in the back of her mind. It's lucky Harvey feels about you the way he does."

Dace lit a cigarette and tossed the match into the fire. She understood what Olivia meant. Harvey had been deeply in love with her for the first year or so, and he had depended on her—but did he now? She was very far from sure. These days of constant stress had made her stop and look and listen, made her think. She would never leave Harvey, but what about him? He had changed in the last year, his need of her had diminished steadily, he went about a great deal by himself—with clients, so he said—and with this new life that would be coming up when this whole unpleasant business about the check was over and everything had been settled, he would have money to burn, money to take him anywhere in the world he wanted to go with any companions he might select. It would be different then, very different. . . . He might want a separation. . . .

Freedom, she thought, with a sudden, wild upsurge, to be free of this idle, empty life to which she had committed herself, that was weighing her down with heavy chains;

77

she would make no effort to break them—but Harvey might. Perhaps he had already talked to Joan Longstreet, confided in her. . . .

She said nothing of this to Olivia, except that there had never been much love lost between herself and Joan. "Well," Olivia said, picking up the slip she was mending and going on with her work, "you'd better watch your step with that fair lady."

Dace glanced sideways at her cousin. Was this an oblique reference to Hugh Clavering? A warning? Could it be? No, Olivia was sewing placidly, and anyhow she was anything but an oblique person; she was simple and direct and said what she had to say plainly. Moreover, she didn't know of the last two meetings with Hugh; Dace dismissed the thought.

Shortly after that a friend of Olivia's called and asked her out to dinner and Dace urged her to go. Now that Harvey had been heard from and she knew he was safe, she didn't mind being alone. She was used to it. But Olivia didn't keep her dinner date. She was upstairs dressing for it when the phone rang again.

This time it was Mr. Bolton, the manager of the Stamford Garage. Harvey had just called Stamford's about the Benz, telling them to fill it with gas and oil and check the tires and have it ready for him down on the street. Bolton said, "When I told Mr. Allert that your Benz wasn't in the garage, he was angry. He told me I was crazy, said it must be, but it isn't, Mrs. Allert. It hasn't been in since one of the boys delivered it to Mr. Allert at your house last Thursday afternoon."

Dace assured the man that it was all right. She said she had the car, that Mr. Allert had been out of town and didn't know it, hung up, and sat staring ahead of her at a silver bowl on the table under the mirror. Harvey wanted the car to drive up to the hospital in—the place was in rather an out-of-the-way spot and not too easily accessible by train. What would he do now, when he couldn't get hold of the Benz? Would he call her, or would he be afraid to call? He had a dim view of the law in any shape, declared in his exaggerated way that all police were thieves and robbers, once he had made her listen to a beep on the phone of a friend who was tangled up in a divorce

78

case—he might even think there was a policeman in the house.

She was back in the living room, walking the floor and trying to figure out what Harvey would do, when the phone rang again. She flew to it. But it wasn't Harvey. It was Scott Evans, and Scott had been drinking—he generally had at that time of day.

"Dace? That you, Dace. . . ? Are you alone?"

Scott spoke like a stage conspirator, in slightly thickened syllables. He wasn't actually drunk but he had an edge on, definitely. She said yes, she was alone, and he said, "Where's the Benz, Dace?"

She told him before she could stop herself, because she was almost instantly suspicious. "Why, Scott? Why do you want to know?"

"Well, it's like this, Dace. I've got to go somewhere in a hurry, see?—and I have no car. Will you do me a favor, will you loan me the Benz? Will you call that garage and have them deliver it here to my place? I can't explain now, but I'll come up to the house later on, as soon as I get back, and tell you all about it."

Dace was thinking rapidly. She said, "All right, Scott," cut short his fervent thanks, and dropped the phone into its cradle. It was Harvey who wanted the car. He was afraid to come here or phone her directly so he had got in touch with Scott. She hadn't the slightest intention of calling the garage. It would be madness. The police knew where the Benz was, the Inspector had taken down the name of the garage Olivia had put it in the other night after Harvey had left it parked outside the gate. The garage was probably being watched, anyhow some sort of check was being kept on the Benz, and the police would simply follow it and grab Harvey. . . .

She got up off the little gilt chair. It was one thing for a wanted man to come forward of his own accord, to say, "Here I am. I understand you want to talk to me"; it was quite another to be caught in what would look like an attempt at flight. It mustn't happen. Harvey would go wild at the ignominy of being seized, without warning, out of a blue sky. He might resist. . . . Shot while attempting to escape—you read about it in the papers all the time. She had to get to Harvey, talk to him. . . . She was at the closet

79

throwing on a coat when Olivia came down the stairs, all aglow.

She paused, a hand on the newel post, looked at Dace with her coat on, and her expression changed. She listened wide-eyed to Dace's account of Scott Evans' phone call, and said practically, "You can't just walk out that door, not if the house is being watched—we don't know that it is but it may be. No . . . First let me call Jim Bates and tell him I can't meet him and then," she thought for a moment, "this is what we'd better do."

Less than five minutes later, after Olivia had made a preliminary reconnaissance, Dace was going down the back stairs on tiptoe like a criminal. The kitchen and pantry doors were closed. In the kitchen a radio was playing and pots and pans were being moved about. The back door was straight ahead. Dace opened it, and closed it soundlessly behind her.

It was snowing again and the visibility was practically zero. You could scarcely see the lighted windows of the houses that fronted on the other streets. Dace fumbled her way over the same route Harvey had taken the other night, through the door in the green wooden fence and into the backyard of the next house. Crossing it the marble statue there gave her a scare. It looked like a man standing watching her. She hurried on through several more gates and across frozen stretches of earth that would be gardens in summer, then down steps and through the dimly lit tunnel of a big apartment house that brought her out on Thirty-sixth Street. A few pedestrians with umbrellas huddled forward against the drive of the wind and the snow, cars and cabs rolling past. She turned east and then south.

She didn't have long to wait in front of the drug store at the corner of Thirty-fifth and Lexington before Olivia came hurrying along. Olivia had kept her eyes open. She had left by the front door and the proper exit from the court, and she was sure she hadn't been followed. Snow sifting down on the pavements, neon signs flashing through it, people hurrying along; there were plenty of cabs but they were all occupied. Olivia said, "We'd better take a bus—here comes one now," and threw up an arm.

They boarded the crowded bus, rode to Fourteenth Street, and walked the rest of the way. It wasn't far. Scott lived on University Place between Tenth and Eleventh Streets. He had a second-floor apartment in which the light of day was never seen. Dace had been there for a drink shortly after her marriage.

Once the slashing brilliance of Fourteenth Street was behind them, University Place was practically in darkness, but she knew the way. Scott's building was in the middle of the block. They mounted snow-covered brownstone steps that led into a dim vestibule, and Dace pressed Scott's bell. He would be expecting the ring, would think it was the man from the garage with the Benz. There was no answering buzz. Dace pressed the bell again and again. Still no answer. The two girls were standing there looking at each other with dismay when Scott Evans spoke.

Scott's voice came from below them, the same conspiratorial voice he had used over the phone. "Hi, Dace. Down here, Dace, in the area."

Dace stepped out on the landing at the top of the steps and looked over the railing. Scott's upturned face was just barely visible through the falling snow. He said anxiously, "Where's the Benz, Dace? I've been waiting for it. You did phone, didn't you? Or did you bring it yourself? Where is it? I want to . . ."

He broke off abruptly. He was no longer looking at her, he had turned and was looking out into the street. Cars lined the curb. Beyond them, in the middle of the street, a car was pulling up opposite the steps. The door opened and two men jumped out. Before they reached the sidewalk Scott Evans was off like a shot in the direction of Tenth Street, his long legs flailing frantically. As he ran he shouted at the top of his lungs. "Help, help . . . Police . . . Help . . ."

The two men who had jumped out of the car pursued Scott at a dead run. They were detectives. He didn't have a chance. They caught him near the next corner, but only after one of them had fired a warning shot in the air. Scott was brought back, struggling as he came. His hat was gone, the sleeve of his overcoat was torn and his tie was under his ear. "Take your hands off me, damn you. Let

81

me go. . . . What the hell is this about?"

"O.K., mister, take it easy now. Just take it easy and you won't get hurt."

Dace and Olivia stood looking on helplessly. They had remained where they were on the steps, immobilized by shock, stunned by it. The suddenness of what had happened and the way it had happened, the open, naked display of force, was an ignominious and sickening spectacle. It was also terrifying.

The two detectives were Benson and Krause from the district attorney's office. Parked in a car on Thirty-sixth Street to stop up the bolt hole there, they had watched Dace emerge from the tunnel under the apartment building. It had been no trick at all to follow her, on and off the bus, and then here to University Place. The surreptitiousness with which she had slipped off had convinced them that she was on her way to meet her husband, the man the office wanted badly to get hold of. They were disappointed and irate when they discovered that the fellow they had bagged was only Harvey Allert's cousin, much as he looked like the wanted man.

Although the neighborhood was sparsely peopled at that time of night, a small crowd had begun to gather: four or five men, several boys and the inevitable woman with a dog. The detectives took Scott Evans and Olivia and Dace inside the house and upstairs to Scott's apartment. It consisted of a kitchen, bedroom, bath and living room. A quick search that included the closets—Dace's muscles unlocked. The search was vain. Harvey wasn't there. The two detectives began asking questions. They questioned Scott first.

"What did you run for if you're in the clear?"

Scott might have had plenty to drink but it didn't appear to have affected his brain; he had all his wits about him. "I didn't know who you were, don't you see—don't you get it? I thought you were a couple of muggers. Didn't you hear me yelling for help, for the police? I wanted to draw you off from my cousin and Miss Wood."

They had no better success with Dace. "You expected to meet your husband here, Mrs. Allert?"

"What gives you that idea?"

"Why did you leave your house by the back way?"

82

"It was shorter, and I often do."

"Your cousin left by the front way and joined you."

"We met by chance and Miss Wood decided to come along with me and see Mr. Evans."

They didn't believe it, but Dace didn't particularly care. The pistol shot out there in the darkness still echoed in her ears. There had been something brutal, nauseating, about Scott's useless flight and his capture, by force. Two against one, two armed men with all the weight of the law. . . . It mustn't happen to Harvey. Harvey must come forward of his own accord, at a time and place of his own choosing.

The telephone was in the bedroom. One of the detectives went in and used it, closing the door behind him. He came out and both men left. When they were alone and Scott had fortified himself with a drink he didn't need, he told them what had happened, his end of it.

Right after Harvey had called the Stamford Garage and found the Benz wasn't there, he had called Scott and asked him to get in touch with Dace and tell her what to do. When the Benz was delivered here by the garage man, Scott was to drive around the block a couple of times to see if it was being tailed. If not, Harvey would pick it up.

Scott nodded and winked, very pleased with himself. "Didn't you hear me yelling? I thought that was pretty good. Harvey said he'd be here but he wouldn't show until it was safe. He couldn't help but hear me giving tongue—and he's had plenty of time to get away by now. God help him if he falls into the hands of those buzzards." He fingered a shoulder gingerly. "All they want to do is make an arrest, that's all they care about."

Scott took another drink, lit a cigarette with a shaky hand and went on walking around. Dace began to notice her surroundings then, for the first time. The apartment had been done over recently. Scott must have got some money somewhere. The old shabbiness had been vastly preferable. The chairs and tables and hangings and lamps were in execrable taste. Everything was too big, too fat and shining and blatant—vulgar. Her eyes went back to Scott. He was restless and overexcited, but there was more than that, there was uneasiness in him. He kept throwing glances at her, pulling hard on his cigarette, and his gestures were aimless, uncoordinated.

Suddenly, in spite of the bright light, the room took on an atmosphere of vague evil. Somehow or other, being in it was like being trapped in an unpleasant place in a nightmare. . . . Her feeling extended to Scott Evans himself. His eyes looked little and mean and his mouth flabby. . . . She had always liked him, had never felt this way about him before. . . . Was he telling the truth? She had a strong feeling that he was not, or not all of it, anyhow.

"Yes," he said, nodding and winking again, "I foxed those bums good and proper. . . . What you've got to do is use the old bean." He took a handkerchief out of his pocket and mopped his face, and as he did so something fluttered to the floor. It was a twenty-dollar bill, a new twenty-dollar bill.

Dace mightn't have noticed it, or if she had she would have thought nothing of it, except for the way Scott stopped and swept the bill up and crammed it back into his pocket hastily, with a quick, darting look at her, a look of apprehension. Instantly she was convinced that twenty-dollar bill was one of the ones with which Harvey's wallet had been stuffed last Thursday. Scott had seen Harvey, been with him. Harvey might even have been staying here . . . .

She said, "Scott, you've been seeing Harvey."

Scott denied it, vehemently. "No, Dace, no—I haven't. I give you my word, I swear to you—I swear to God . . ."

"All right, Scott, all right," she said wearily.

He was lying and lying badly, but Harvey was obviously not in the apartment now and there was nothing to do but go home. Gallant to the last, although he was distinctly shaken, Scott pressed drinks on them out of his small remaining supply and when they refused he went out, hailed a cab, and put them into it.

There was news waiting for them when they got back to the house on Murray Hill. Gerald Straws was in the living room drifting around aimlessly, his hands deep in his pockets, a cold pipe between his teeth.

Elfrida was dead.

EIGHT

Dace's suspicions about Scott Evans had a solid founda-
tion in fact. The two men from the district attorney's office
hadn't immediately left the building. When Olivia and
Dace went they were still there questioning the tenants.
They hit the jack pot with a Miss Beardsley on the third
floor. Miss Beardsley had seen a man answering Harvey
Allert's description—as near enough as didn't matter
—enter Scott Evans' apartment earlier that evening,
about an hour before the contretemps down in the street
in the snow-filled darkness. She hadn't seen the man's
face—his back was to her as he went through Scott Evans'
door and closed it behind him—but he was the proper
height, etc., and had on a light tan tweed coat with the
collar turned up. Moreover, Miss Beardsley had seen the
same man half a dozen times before—at least he looked
like the same man she saw tonight—arriving at those wild
parties Scott Evans gave, with girls and loud music and
racketing until the small hours. You couldn't hear your
ears and you couldn't get any sleep. It was disgraceful,
and you could smell the liquor as far down as the front
door.

Shown an enlargement of one of the snapshots McKee
had taken from the house in the court on Murray Hill,

Miss Beardsley identified Harvey as Scott Evans' visitor both that night and on previous occasions.

To establish Harvey Allert as having been in Evans' apartment earlier that evening was one thing. As far as tracing him away from it to wherever he had gone when he took to his heels, warned by Evans' shouts and his pseudoflight, the two detectives had no success whatever. Even if Harvey Allert had succeeded in getting hold of his car and driving up to the hospital in Putnam in it, he wouldn't have been in time to see his stepmother alive. Elfrida Allert died at seven-fifteen P.M.

That was on Saturday night. On Sunday Dwyer saw McKee briefly. Dwyer had by no means given up on the forgery charge against Allert but he wasn't as belligerent as he had been at the start. All three experts who examined the thousand-dollar check, signed with Elfrida Allert's name and cashed by her stepson, agreed that it was a forgery. Two of them believed that Allert was the forger, and that the forging had been done with the smaller of the two pens removed from Allert's desk in the Murray Hill house. The third disagreed in toto.

"Beginning to weaken, are you?" McKee asked, and Dwyer said, "I most certainly am not. But"—he added gloomily—"the woman's dead and Allert's now the possessor of better than a cool million and a half, and if he sticks to his denial he can hire a battery of handwriting biggies—and you know what that means. We'll have a fight on our hands. The trouble is Beecham. He's breathing down the back of my neck, he wants action, in a hurry."

McKee said, "Tell him to go jump in the lake."

The examination of Elfrida's car had been completed, and just as the Scotsman had foreseen, no definite conclusion one way or the other was possible. If any tampering with the car had been done in advance, the smash-up had wiped out the evidence of it. Had the car remained comparatively intact, there might have been a hope, but it was a complete wreck.

Dwyer said, "Beecham swears Allert killed his stepmother as sure as God made little apples."

McKee was uninterested. "Could be—but it's not for us, Dwyer. I wouldn't touch it with a ten-foot pole."

"So the fellow's just to walk out of hiding and rake in the shekels—Beecham's sure he'll put in an appearance now that Elfrida's dead and the money is there waiting for him." McKee said, "Maybe," and Dwyer said, "What do you mean, maybe? What's the good of all that dough if he doesn't claim it? What use will it be to him if he can't lay a finger on it?"

McKee shrugged. "The money's not going to run away, and if your men are right and Allert was down there on University Place last night when they grabbed Evans —well, as far as Harvey Allert's coming forward voluntarily goes, it was the worst possible thing that could have happened. The very worst. He can't be in any doubt now of what's in store for him if he does show. He seems to have been going to try and put in an appearance up there at the hospital, possibly to try it out and see what would happen. Well, he saw all right."

That was on Sunday. McKee had plenty of work to occupy him and no official stake in the Allert affair whatever, but on the following Tuesday morning a piece of interesting information came into the office. The bank at which Elfrida Allert's thousand-dollar check had been cashed had been able to come up with the serial numbers of more than a good half of the bills given to Harvey Allert. Five hundred and eighty dollars in twenty-dollar bills had come out of a fresh package of new money, tapped by the cashier to make up the thousand and shoved under the window to Harvey Allert. The usual routine in all such cases had been put in motion, and that morning one of the twenty-dollar bills given to Allert had turned up. Half an hour later McKee rang Scott Evans' doorbell.

From inside the apartment Evans shouted, "Come in," and McKee did so.

Scott Evans was in the living room tying his bow tie in front of a mirror. Dapper Dan—he was very particular about the set of the tie. He was dressing to go to Elfrida Allert's funeral She was to be buried beside her husband in the small cemetery up in Duchess County near the Allert farm that afternoon.

It was early, not yet ten A.M.; Scott was sober and consequently in a bad humor. He resented being questioned but McKee went on boring in pleasantly.

What Dace Allert had suspected concerning her husband was so; Harvey Allert had been in Evans' apartment on last Saturday night.

Evans didn't give willingly, he had to be prodded. He denied it at first, vigorously—speaking his piece with gestures. "You're barking up the wrong tree, Inspector. I haven't seen old Harve in more than a week. I don't know anything about him, where he is now or what he's doing—anything at all. Yes, yes, yes, I know he phoned me. I told those detectives that the other night, but I have no idea where he is at the present moment and it's no use your asking me. I can't tell you what I don't know, can I?"

McKee produced the twenty-dollar bill that was one of the ones given to Harvey Allert by the bank. He said so. "Mr. Evans, you bought two bottles of Scotch at the Graham Liquor Store on Fourteenth Street yesterday at noon and paid for them with this bill."

"All right, all *right*."

Evans did talk then. He was anxious to get it over with, he had to catch a train. Harvey had been in the apartment Saturday evening. Evans wasn't there when he came, he was having a couple at the Allbright bar down the street. Harvey came while he was out.

"How did he get in?" McKee asked, and Evans said, "Oh, he has a key," looked uncomfortable, and threw out a hand with one of his sweeping movements.

Dace was a peach, there was no one who admired and looked up to her more than he did, but—well, Harvey was different. A fellow like Harve liked a bit of fun once in a while, off the reservation—and what a wife didn't know wouldn't hurt her. The girls Harve had here were the kind that wouldn't make any trouble, they were just out for a good time. There was nothing serious about it, absolutely not—it didn't mean a thing. Sometimes, too, Harvey would bring a couple of chaps along for a game. . . . He hoped Dace wouldn't have to know, he really was crazy about her. . . . He went on with his story.

When Harvey didn't find him there he left. Evans was only back a little while when Harvey phoned him and gave him instructions about Dace and the car, what to tell her to do. He wanted the Benz so he could drive up and see Elfrida, he didn't know then that the poor old girl was already dead. Harvey had left two twenties for him under the clock, he was a generous lad, quick on the draw, there wasn't a mean bone in his body, and he never asked you to do something for nothing. . . .

"And after the Benz was delivered here you were to turn it over to him when you'd driven it around the block a couple of times?"

Evans nodded belligerently. "That's right. Why not? Anything wrong about it? It was his own car."

A pity, McKee reflected, that Dwyer's men hadn't held back and waited a bit the other night. "You know that your cousin is wanted by the police for forgery, Mr. Evans."

Dashing a glass of milk liberally with brandy, Evans made a rude noise. "That's hogwash. Now that Elfrida's dead who's going to prosecute, go after Harvey with the law?"

McKee studied the man. In spite of the liquor there were brains left under that mournful and pathetic basset hound exterior, and Scott Evans had reason to be grateful to the Allerts. His mother had been the old man's sister. He had been sent through the university by Harvey père and more or less brought up with Harvey Junior and generally taken care of for years, until he finally put himself beyond the pale by his drinking and his general shiftlessness. He'd do anything for Harvey Allert he could—it might pay to keep an eye on Evans.

McKee returned to the office thinking about Beecham's insistence that there was proof somewhere of Harvey Allert's rigging of his stepmother's death by doing something to her car that had brought about her crash. Beecham said she was an unusually fast driver and liked to go. McKee himself had no opinion on the subject. Maybe yes and maybe no; certainly there was nothing now on which Homicide could move. But just in case something did eventually break, it would be as well to keep informed as to what went on. Besides Scott Evans, Mercedes Allert, her cousin Olivia Wood, the Kermit Longstreets, Gerald Straws and Hugh Clavering were either on their way or already at the farm in Duchess County for Elfrida Allert's funeral. It was scarcely likely that Harvey Allert would turn up there with the forgery rap hanging over his head, but you never knew. Back behind his desk McKee pulled the phone toward him and called the local state police barracks in that part of Duchess, and put his request.

Meanwhile Dace and Olivia had already left New York. Gerald Straws drove them up to the farm in his car, an old Rolls Harvey had picked up for him for almost nothing. The Rolls, Dace thought, was typical of Gerald and of his fastidious selectivity. He didn't like many things, but what he had he wanted to be good. He lived in a run-down house on Jones Street because he liked the shape of the rooms and the neighborhood, and some of the few pieces the place contained could have found a place in a museum.

For the most part the long drive was a silent one through a winter world of white snow and dark trees under a leaden sky. No one said very much—they had talked themselves out. Dace had broken down briefly the other night. When they got back to the house from Scott's and found Gerald there with the news that Elfrida was dead she had wept uncontrollably. Olivia had said wonderingly in her downright way, "But Dace—you knew she was going to die." It wasn't only for Elfrida, or even principally for her, that Dace had wept. The nightmare quality of the whole episode down there in the darkness and the falling snow on University Place haunted her. Perhaps she *had* been a bad wife, perhaps Joan Longstreet was right—it wasn't to her Harvey had turned for aid and comfort when he needed it, it was to Scott Evans he had gone. Harvey was afraid of her. . . . The thought was a lance cutting into her. Poor Harvey, driven by fear of her, his wife, and also of the police.

Gerald had been kind to her and gentle, but as always, aloof, looking at her thoughtfully with those light eyes of his you could never get behind, and saying, "Let her alone, Olivia. Go ahead and cry, Dace, it will do you good," upon which of course she had abruptly stopped. She hadn't wanted to come up to Duchess County—she hadn't known Elfrida well and she was only a relative by marriage—but the other two had persuaded her. One of the reasons why she hadn't wanted to come was Hugh Clavering. She knew now that in spite of what she had told herself, where Hugh was concerned her vaunted indifference was a myth. She hadn't really got over him, she had tried to get over him by marrying Harvey, and it not only hadn't been a success, it had been a tragic failure. All she had succeeded in doing was in pulling Harvey down and destroying him. He knew instinctively that she didn't love him—with all his faults he was abnormally sensitive—and that was where the dry rot had begun.

What talk there was during the two-and-a-half-hour drive was done by Gerald and Olivia. It was desultory, idle. Olivia speculated on what Elfrida had done with her personal fortune, she had lived simply, considering her income and must have piled up a sizeable estate. Also the farm was Elfrida's and she could do what she liked with it. Joan Longstreet thought she'd leave everything to Hugh Clavering and Gerald said probably, with a provision for Madge Tarbel. Like everyone else he was fond of Madge. When he and Harvey were boys they had spent a good deal of time at the farm and Madge had always been a good skate, helping them out of scrapes and hiding their misdemeanors from the eagle eye of Harvey's father.

Dace had been at the Duchess County place last summer and her eye began to pick up landmarks after they turned north at Millbrook and started up the valley. The ten-acre field first, then the pine woods, then the house itself, long and low and white with a barn attached, set high on a shoulder of one of the rolling hills against a background of the mountains on the other side of the river. Gerald sent the Rolls through the gates and up the driveway, and then they were there.

Getting out, Olivia said anxiously, "Do I look all right, Dace?" She didn't own a black coat and Dace had made her wear her broadtail. Full length on her, on Olivia it made a three-quarter coat with push-up sleeves. She said perfunctorily, "Very nice, Olivia," and they started up the steps. Hugh was the first person Dace saw when they went in.

He was in the huge hall that ran clear to the roof and was used as a living room, standing in front of the fireplace you could roast an ox in. He was wearing a dark suit with a black tie that made him look strange, formal and older. She had dreaded this meeting before others, before Gerald particularly with his clear, ruminative gaze that missed nothing, ever—and it was unexpectedly easy. She might have been anyone.

Hugh had been very fond of Elfrida and her death had saddened him. He shook hands decorously with all three of them in turn. The appropriate, meaningless things were said and done, and their coats and hats carried off and put in the cedar closet under the stairs by Gerald. "That's all right, Clavering, I'll take them, I know my way around." Hugh said they were short of help and the house was at sixes and sevens—it had been closed since Elfrida's accident—but as it was needed for only one day that didn't matter. Elfrida was to be buried at three o'clock that afternoon.

Four hours to go, Dace thought. How are we ever going to get through them? Gerald had insisted in his calm way on starting early for fear that the roads might be bad or they might have a breakdown. Then Madge Tarbel appeared. Madge's eyes were swollen with crying and the tip of her nose was red. Of all the people in the house, Dace reflected later, Hugh and Madge were the only ones who felt any real sorrow. She and Elfrida had been very close and Elfrida had no relatives except a couple of distant cousins in another part of the world.

Madge was a simple soul, kindly; she had evidently been briefed about Harvey in some sort of fashion, probably by Hugh, and she didn't say anything about him. "Mercedes, dear." She kissed Dace and said it was good of her to come, Olivia, too—"And I knew we could depend on you, Gerald. Would you all like to come in here for a moment?" Elfrida filled her thoughts. She waved at a door to the right. "She was only brought home this morning. The casket's closed, you know—they decided it was better. . . . Poor Elfrida." Her tears ran.

They paid a brief visit to the long double drawing room on the right. It was filled with flowers. Madge insisted on showing Dace her violets and the Longstreets' roses and Scott Evans' basket of chrysanthemums, then they went back to the hall. People were beginning to arrive and Hugh and Madge and Gerald were busy. They knew these friends and neighbors of Elfrida's; Dace didn't. Olivia had disappeared somewhere. Going into the kitchen for a glass

92

of water, Dace found her there eating a sandwich and chatting with the farmer's wife, Mrs. Neibold, who had come over from the cottage to help out.

Olivia was in raptures over the kitchen and the utility room beyond it, all Monel metal and pale green tiles, the great stove flush with the wall, besides an immense Deep-Freeze, a huge refrigerator and endless shining counters. She said, "It's magnificent, Dace, isn't it, after New York kitchens—particularly my hole in the wall. Hugh will have to get himself a wife, this is absolutely wasted on a man." Mrs. Neibold, the farmer's wife, said that Mrs. Allert had loved her kitchen, for all her money she liked to do things for herself, and enjoyed puttering about. Poor soul . . . Dace left them chatting, got her coat, and slipped unobtrusively through the door at the foot of the back stairs.

It was gray out, the skies were lower, and the bite of the wind was keen. You could see your breath, but it was good to feel the icy air on one's face, to be alone and not to have to talk to anyone. She walked down the shoveled path toward the pine woods that came close in on the north, thinking of Harvey. Gerald didn't believe he would come here and neither did she, not after what had happened down on University Place in New York the other night. No, Harvey wouldn't come here, and yet he was given to bravura gestures. Striking an attitude filled some need in him, a demand for excitement, drama.

She had put the house well behind her and was standing still looking at Stissing, the first of the Berkshires, through a gap in the trees when she heard the footsteps behind her. Harvey, she thought, and whirled around with a gasp. It wasn't Harvey, it was Hugh.

A topcoat swung from his shoulders. He had no hat on. Wind ruffled his dark hair. He stood looking at her, his eyes brilliant under his sharply etched black brows. His grave formality was gone. When he looked like this he was dangerous.

"Did I frighten you, Dace?"

His voice was different, too. . . . She gathered herself together. "No—yes."

He went on deliberately. "I saw you come out and followed you." Then he was close to her, holding her two

93

hands, crushing them in his. "Dace, Dace." His voice was a cry, a demand. "How long is this to go on? It's killing you. Give it up. You don't love Harvey, it's your conscience. . . . And it isn't any use. Harvey will be all right. There's nothing you can do for him. Now that he's come into his own he won't need you. He'll give you a divorce. . . . Dace, you must. We belong together, it's the only way we can live. I know it and you know it. We were fools once, but we know now, both of us. . . ."

What Hugh said was true, Dace thought swiftly. Thought? Felt. It was a beat in her blood. Harvey didn't need her, he had no further use for her, she was simply excess baggage, an unwanted burden he had outgrown. He would be glad to be free of her, freedom was what he wanted, to be tied to no one, to come and go as he pleased. . . .

For a moment, standing there in the snow, she was sorely tempted. It was only for a moment. Then the gray chill of sanity was back in her. You couldn't throw off bonds that were unbreakable, nor could you recapture the past, make it live again as though nothing had intervened. Too much had happened. What she and Hugh had once had was gone, irretrievably. Harvey stood between them, the good times with him as well as the bad. She was different now, and so was Hugh, even if he didn't know it.

"Dace, answer me," he said. "Tell me you'll leave Harvey. Tell me . . ."

"Hugh, don't . . . Stop."

She took her hands out of his, took a step back. Hugh let her go. His face changed. His mouth was compressed, his eyes a dark burn. He stared at her fixedly. Then he smiled. It wasn't a pleasant smile. She could feel the anger in him, it reached out and scorched her, as he said slowly, "I suppose I have got a nerve asking you to give up what you'll have now that Elfrida's dead, what you've won through to. . . . I'm a poor man."

There was scorn in him and self-derision. He was trying to hurt her because he was suffering himself. Dace held herself stiffly around inner shakiness.

"It's not the money, Hugh—you know that."

"Then what is it?" he demanded. "Don't tell me you love Harvey. . . ?"

94

He stopped abruptly. A sudden, soft shush shattered the winter stillness. It came from close by. It was snow sliding from the branches of a clump of firs beyond the turn where the path disappeared into the woods. *Harvey,* Dace thought again, her heart pounding; Harvey was there out of sight watching them, listening to them—and knew she was being absurd. But there was someone coming up the path—snow squeaked under leather. It was Gerald Straws.

He came walking out from among the trees, hands in the pockets of a heavy mackinaw he had found somewhere, the inevitable pipe between his teeth. He wore it as another man might wear a decoration. He joined them. His greeting was pleasant, casual. "Hi, Clavering, out for a breather? Dace, you'll catch your death in those shoes, it must be near zero—you should have put boots on."

Dace pulled her coat tighter around her, cold with a coldness that had nothing to do with the thermometer. Had Gerald overheard her and Hugh talking, heard what they said? She could tell nothing from his face as they walked back to the house together with Hugh in the lead. Hugh was in control of himself again, at least outwardly. He left them abruptly in the small square hall at the foot of the back stairs and Dace was about to follow when Gerald said to her, "Wait a minute, will you?" He hung the mackinaw up on one of a row of hooks and turned to her. His light eyes, fastened on her face, studying it, were thoughtful.

"Dace, if I were you I'd be careful."

She looked past him in the dim light. So Gerald had heard, he must have . . . He spoke slowly putting a lot of meaning into the words. . . . What difference did it make whether he had heard or not? If he chose to think she was playing around with Hugh and that her anxiety about Harvey was a mockery, pretense and nothing but pretense, let him—anyhow there was nothing she could do about it.

"Careful?" she asked coldly, her brows raised.

Gerald nodded amiably. "You're far too trusting, you know—you take everything and everyone on faith. If the surface looks all right, that's the way it is." He shook his head. "You're making a mistake."

Was he warning her about Hugh on general principles, or was he constituting himself her mentor, as Harvey's friend, giving her a little lecture on deportment? "I don't know what you're talking about."

"I realize you don't, I'll tell you. You were being watched all the time you were outside. There's a state trooper out there in the grounds keeping an eye wide open, possibly there's more than one. They're probably waiting to see if Harvey will turn up. . . ." Gerald wasn't himself either. He added with muted violence, putting a clenched fist against the newel post, just touching it and drawing his fist away again, "I wish to God he would. I wish he'd drive up to the front door openly and walk in."

Harvey didn't turn up at the front door. He manifested himself in an entirely different fashion a little later on in the day. Before that Joan Longstreet was proved entirely wrong about the disposition of Elfrida's estate, and something of Beecham's attitude, if not palliated, was at least partially explained.

NINE

Beyond an annuity to Madge Tarbel and a cash legacy to Mr. and Mrs. Neibold, the farmer and his wife who took care of the estate, Elfrida had left everything of which she died possessed to Harvey. It was Madge who told Dace about it, upstairs in her own room over the tea and sandwiches Dace had insisted on bringing her at shortly before one o'clock, she looked so tired.

"Yes," she said in the face of Dace's astonishment, "yes. Elfrida had a conscience that—it wore her out. I don't think she'd have been killed if she hadn't been such a worrier. She was always thinking and thinking and not paying attention to what went on around her. Scruples—balancing this way and that, over and over again. She'd say, 'It's not what you want to do, Madge, it's what you *should* do.'"

So that was what Hugh meant when he said that about being a poor man, Dace thought. Did he, could he believe that it was because of money that she wouldn't leave Harvey? "But Hugh Clavering," she said aloud, "I would have supposed—Elfrida was very fond of him, and she depended on him—and this house and the money she accumulated out of her income were her own to do as she liked with. . . ."

Madge shook her head and drank some tea. "She didn't figure that way. She figured it had all come from Harvey's father, everything, and it should go back to Harvey when she died. Hugh knew about it, she told him when she was in New York this last time. I was there in the hotel, I came up only two days before the accident to get this place in shape for the winter. If only I hadn't—if only I'd been with her . . ." Madge suppressed tears. "Hugh was real angry with her when she tried to explain."

"Angry?" Dace lit a cigarette.

Madge nodded. "Yes, indeed he was. He asked Elfrida in that curt way he has sometimes why she thought she had to explain at all. He did make her feel better, just the same I know she wanted to leave him money and it bothered her—but she was like that—she did, not what she wanted to do herself, but what she made up her mind was the right thing, the thing that ought to be done. And yet with it all she worried about Harvey having so much, what he'd do, what would happen to him. If I told her once I told her fifty times that he was free, white and going on for forty, and that you couldn't live other people's lives for them no matter how hard you tried or how much you wanted to." Madge paused and looked at Dace. "There's nothing really wrong—with Harvey, I mean? Hugh told me there was a little trouble and that Harvey wouldn't be here. It's nothing—serious, is it, Mercedes?"

Why trouble her needlessly, she was fond of Harvey. Dace said, "He's gotten himself into a bit of a mess, but it'll work out," and Madge nodded incuriously. "He was always one for getting into scrapes," she said, and lapsed into reminiscence, and presently when Dace had made her finish the pot of tea they went downstairs.

Elfrida had been a prominent figure in the community of farms and estates flung over the hills and by that time people had begun arriving in force. Interested glances were cast at Dace as the wife of the heir to the Allert estate, and four or five people came up to her and asked about Harvey. "Mr. Allert's here?" To each one Dace gave the same answer, "Not just now." Watching these decorous, upright, rather prosy men and women, and talking to them, she could understand Harvey's not

98

wanting to face the countryside with a charge of forgery hanging over his head.

More and more flowers kept coming. At around two o'clock Dace was standing alone near the fire when the blanket of daisies was delivered. Its size, and the purity of its crisp white and gold, caught her eye as the farmer's wife carried it off. Olivia was over near the door helping out by collecting the cards so that they could be acknowledged later. She crossed the crowded room to Dace, a card in her hand. Her eyes were round behind her glasses.

It was Harvey who had sent the blanket of daisies.

"Look at this." Olivia showed Dace the card. The message on it was brief, just "To Elfrida from Harvey." That was all.

Dace didn't move and she didn't speak. She couldn't. The room was unsteady, out of focus. She stared ahead of her at a group of wavering backs, the long fold of a mink coat. Shortly after his father's death and on more than one occasion later Harvey had said, "We've got nothing to worry about, not a thing—Elfrida'll soon be pushing up the daisies."

Pushing up the daisies . . . Dace's stomach churned. The blanket of spring flowers was a savage indecency, the flaunted triumph of a death wish that had achieved fulfillment. . . . Elfrida hadn't died soon, she had grown stronger, healthier, with an increased life expectancy until, unexpectedly and dreadfully, she had been killed as the result of a fatal accident. An accident, an accident, an accident . . . The words repeated themselves over and over in Dace's brain, a somber and ghastly fugue from which escape was impossible, twist and turn and try to stop her ears as she might.

Harvey hadn't been reticent about how he felt or what he thought, in those early days immediately following his father's death. He had kept up a good face in public but he had talked freely enough in private, when he was with Gerald and Olivia, among others. . . .

Gerald had joined them beside the hearth without her noticing. He was examining the card. She looked at him. Pushing up the daisies . . . Did he, did Olivia remember, too, as she did? There was no way of telling. There was no

99

way of telling anything—she had thought she knew Harvey inside and out, and she didn't know him at all. The surface, yes, what he showed her, but nothing more. While he had pretended to be cheerful, philosophic, had a festering hatred of Elfrida been gathering in him, and had it . . . ? Dace started to put an aimless hand to her forehead.

Gerald's voice brought her back. At her side he said warningly in a low voice, "Watch it, Dace. . . . Harvey's flowers were probably wired. I'm going to phone and see what I can find out."

Dace's vision cleared. The room settled back into place. Joan Longstreet was coming up to her under full sail, in smart, floating black and a tiny hat with the suggestion of a veil on it. She knew about Elfrida's will, that Elfrida had left Harvey everything including the farm, Madge had told her, and she was glowing with satisfaction and pleasure, all her teeth flashing. Elfrida was wonderful. . . . They had certainly misjudged her, hadn't they—and Hugh Clavering, too. . . . She had just been having a chat with him, he was really a charming man when you got to know him better. . . . It simply went to show what prejudice would do—so stupid really, it was just that she herself was so jealous of Harvey's interests. Poor, darling boy, it was a pity he couldn't have been here, he had been so fond of, so devoted to Elfrida, but under the circumstances—that dreadful man Beecham—better not. But Harvey had sent flowers. Had Dace seen them? They were lovely, so fresh. . . . Her roses had been a mistake, too soft. . . . Ah, there was the senator with his wife, she had dined with them last year in this very house. They would want to meet Dace . . . .

After that there wasn't far to go. The time finally wore itself out and then there was only the interment to face. The drive from the house, between snow-covered fields and dark woods under a dark sky, was a short one. Charles Beecham was in the cemetery. He stood across from Dace in the front ranks of the crowd on the other side of the grave, big and commanding in a black overcoat and black hat and a white scarf. The long bronze casket banked with flowers was between them. Harvey's offering lay across the top, a brilliant white and gold in the gloomy

100

light. An icy wind ruffled the petals that covered Elfrida's body. Pushing up—the daisies . . . Dace looked away from it—and straight into the lawyer's eyes.

They were invisible behind rounds of glittering crystal fixed on her steadily, as though Beecham was gazing contemplatively into her mind, examining its contents. A deep shudder went through her. She had a frantic impulse to back away, turn and run; she stood stiffly still, her hands tight inside the sable muff Madge Tarbel had insisted on her carrying because of the bitter cold, a muff that had belonged to the dead woman. After they returned to the house Beecham talked to her.

"I am as anxious as you are that Harvey should come home, Mr. Beecham, I can assure you of that," Dace said, sitting quiet in a small armchair, her back to the window. "I can only repeat that I don't know where he is. If I did I would certainly tell you."

"Oh, yes, naturally, naturally—of course, Mrs. Allert."

The two of them were alone together in the little writing room at the rear of the hall. Beecham took a thoughtful stroll up and down the floor, hands clasped meditatively behind his back. Sweetness and light and a desire to be of help—his manner was bland, paternalistic. There was no sign of his bitterness at Harvey, his determination to ruin him. There wouldn't be. Beecham wouldn't show his cards to her, Dace thought. He knew all about Harvey's attempt to get hold of the Benz last Saturday night, through Scott Evans. She had seen them together—and Scott had been wax in Beecham's hands. He had explained as an opener that it was now his business, his official business, as an executor of Elfrida's estate, to find Harvey without delay. He also knew about the flowers that had come here.

He paused close to her. "You didn't send them in Harvey's name, Mrs. Allert?"

"I did not."

Did Beecham think she and Olivia and Gerald Straws were all trying to cover up for Harvey, pretending, for instance, that he was in New York while actually he was far away? She told the lawyer what Gerald had found out. Harvey had ordered the flowers himself over the phone from Rustecks', the shop they always used, the people who supplied flowers for the Murray Hill house. "If you

101

doubt me," Dace said, "you can talk to Rustecks' yourself."

"My dear Mrs. Allert . . ." Beecham was gently reproachful, and benevolent. Surely she could understand his anxiety, things were at a standstill, and there were decisions to be made, a number of decisions, and letters of administration to be applied for. . . .

Dace said, emphasizing each word with cold precision, that if the charge about the check hadn't been made to the police and a warrant for his arrest issued, Harvey would have been home long ago.

Ah yes, the check—but there were other people involved. . . . If it was simply the check perhaps some arrangement could be made. . . . "You think it's the check that's keeping him—in, ah—hiding?"

Beecham's big white face was fixed in an expression of frowning consideration, not too grave, merely speculative, considering. The glasses were turned full on her; he was watching her closely. An accident, an accident . . . The blanket of daisies—an open and callous expression of triumph, a last laugh? Say it with flowers? Nightmare was around her again. She pulled herself clear. She could be wrong, this could be only a fantasy, an idea in her mind. One thing was certain—she must not show fear.

She said aloud, "The check, yes, that certainly—and there may be other things keeping him away . . ." and looked down.

She had had a few words with Scott Evans herself earlier, a miserable, muttering, embarrassed Scott, enough to tell her the truth about the many nights Harvey had supposedly been out on business entertaining clients until morning—which was no real shock to her. If Beecham knew about Scott's rooms and the girls and what had gone on there, let him suppose that that was at the bottom of the strain in her, the tension she couldn't hide.

Apparently she succeeded. From his expression she could tell that the lawyer knew very well to what she was alluding. He looked uncomfortable and hemmed and hawed and said that grown men did make idiots of themselves sometimes, but that it meant nothing, and returned to business with a glance at his watch. He would do his part, the moment he discovered anything he would get in touch with her, and he hoped she would do the same by him—as for the police, they would be called off, at once. She could make her mind easy about that, rely on it absolutely. Meanwhile, in any other way at all, he was completely at her service. He bent over her hand and went.

Half an hour later Madge Tarbel and Olivia and Dace were alone in the house. Earlier in the afternoon Madge had asked Dace whether she couldn't stay over until tomorrow. She herself was going to a niece in Vermont for a month but before she went there were a number of things to be decided. She said, "It'll be lonely here tonight—just the first night, you know." Her patience and her quiet sorrow were touching, and after consulting with Olivia, who said it was all right with her, Dace agreed.

The removal of the sword hanging over Harvey's head was an enormous relief, and for the first time in days and days her life began to take on an almost normal cast. The warrant for Harvey's arrest to be withdrawn, quashed, made null and void; now he could come home without the fear of a hand on his shoulder, of the ignominy and shame of being arrested for a criminal offense. It lightened her spirits, a little anyhow, and gave her fresh strength. On his way to his car Beecham had had a word with Kermit Longstreet, and the rejoicing that Harvey was out of the woods and his troubles over was general.

Joan Longstreet said triumphantly, "I knew that that ridiculous charge would never stand up, never, that they couldn't *possibly* make it stick. Now Beecham and the police have found that out for themselves and they're making a virtue of necessity—after stirring up all this trouble and putting Harvey through hell—but anyhow, it's over." Kermit was relieved, too, in his quieter way. So was Scott Evans. "Harve ought to get after the police—what? Maybe at that he should have let them grab him and then sue them for false arrest. That'd teach them."

Shortly after that they all went, in a body. Dace had scarcely spoken to Hugh since that scene at the edge of the pine woods that had been cut short by the appearance of Gerald Straws. His shield back in place, his manner perfectly normal, she couldn't tell what he was thinking, feeling. She would have liked to have had one little word with him, just one, alone, but she couldn't. She said good-bye to him under a battery of eyes. "Good-bye, Hugh." "Good-bye, Dace—I'm glad Beecham's seeing the light." "Yes." And that was all. Hatted and furred, Joan smiled on everyone in her most overwhelming manner, even Scott Evans, helping himself to a last drink to celebrate. She was particularly cordial to Hugh. Dace must bring Mr. Clavering to see them soon, she'd arrange something —yes.

Gerald Straws went last, and it was Gerald who struck a sour note in the universal air of relief, relaxation. Pausing at the door and pulling on his gloves, he said, "Don't get your hopes up too high, Dace. Calling off the police is all very well—it's fine—but we can't very well put an ad in the papers. How in blazes is Harvey going to *know* about it, how is he going to find out?"

It was an angle Dace hadn't thought about and after the door closed behind Gerald she returned frowningly to the fire. How *would* Harvey find out that he no longer had anything to fear from the police? Olivia said cheerfully, "Don't look so cast down. Gerald Straws is crazy. He always looks on the dark side, always expects the worst. It's getting to be a habit with him—he's a real prophet of doom. Harvey will call you, or he'll call Gerald or Scott Evans. That's what will happen—you wait and see."

It was a little after four o'clock when Gerald drove off. Denuded of people and voices and movement the big house seemed very still and very empty. While they were at the cemetery the mortician's men had swept away every vestige of death. There wasn't so much as a flower petal left, and that, in some odd way, seemed to make Elfrida more alive, as though she might walk in through one of the doors and begin to speak. No wonder Madge hadn't wanted to be alone here, Dace thought.

There wasn't much she or Olivia could do, or Madge herself for the matter of that. She had never really unpacked. She had only come up from New York two days before Elfrida's crash, and as soon as she got word of what had happened to Elfrida she had gone down and stayed at a hotel within reaching distance of the hospital, only returning for the funeral the night before. Beecham had explained that everything would have to be left as it was for the appraisers. Elfrida's jewels were in the bank, except the ones she had been wearing, and Beecham had taken care of those. Most of her furs were in storage.

Joining the two girls in the living room after half an hour upstairs alone, Madge said she thought she'd leave the next day for her niece's in Vermont. There was nothing to closing the house. Mrs. Neibold would come over and clear out the refrigerator and put dust covers on the furniture and see that all the doors and windows were locked, that was all. The house would be ready for Dace and Harvey at any time they decided to use, it, and there was nothing to keep her there. After Beecham's pronouncement to the Longstreets, Madge had had to be told about the check and the charge that Harvey had forged it. She returned to the subject hesitatingly.

Madge hadn't been taken in by Joan Longstreet. She didn't express an opinion one way or the other but she said that if Harvey had forged any check, in a way she could understand it. Elfrida had tried to hold him on too tight a rein. "Harvey's always been like that. I remember some of the fights he used to have with his father. . . . You had to use tactics, coax him, you could never drive him, it made him go wild." Of Beecham she said rather surprisingly that she thought he and Elfrida might just possibly have married if Elfrida had lived. Elfrida was used to having a man around, and she was lonely.

Olivia said that maybe that was why Beecham had been so nasty, he was out of luck in all directions. He'd lose the handling of the estate now, too. Kermit Longstreet would be Harvey's lawyer and would take care of his affairs.

Madge was the most charitable of women but it was evident she didn't care very much for Joan Longstreet. "So that's why she was looking so pleased. I never knew a woman to ask so many questions, how much did this place cost to keep up, what were the taxes, did the farm pay? She insisted on looking everywhere, even in the hen houses. Oh well, I suppose you can't blame her for being glad about her husband's getting more business—but haven't the Longstreets got a lot of money, Dace? She works, doesn't she, and gets a big salary?"

Dace said twenty-five thousand a year, but the Longstreets lived up to every cent, and were always crying

105

poverty, or at least Joan was.

Olivia stretched her long legs out in front of her and linked her hands behind her head. "Did you get that bit of byplay about Hugh Clavering, Dace? That woman's a schemer if ever there was one. Remember what I said—I know it sounds absurd but that's what's in her mind. She'd like nothing better than to see you take off with Hugh, or anyone else—I don't think it would much matter who—and leave her a clear field. It really was rather raw . . . ."

Olivia spoke idly. Thinking of what had passed during her brief walk outside earlier in the day, Dace could feel her color begin to rise. But neither of the others was looking at her. She got to her feet. "Joan's not worth thinking about. . . . I'm going out for a walk."

Olivia went with her. It would have been pleasant to wander over the fields, but the snow was too deep so they had to confine themselves to the grounds where the paths were shoveled or cleared with a tractor. They didn't stay out long, the wind was sharp and the light was beginning to draw down. On the way back they stopped for a chat with Tom Neibold, who ran the farm, a stocky middle-aged man with a broad, weather-beaten face. He was working around just inside the huge barn that housed the farm implements, tractors and a plow and cultivators, and the cars, a black and white station wagon, and Madge's neat little coupé.

Neibold spoke of Elfrida and then of Harvey. Terrible thing about Mrs. Allert, terrible, they all felt it badly, she was a good, kind lady and gave you a free hand. Too bad Mr. Harvey was away, but he supposed they'd be seeing him when he got back and they got home themselves. He and his wife were going on their vacation—at that time of year there wasn't much doing on the farm—but his brother-in-law would be at the cottage and in charge if Mr. Harvey wanted to get in touch with him.

Dace thanked him and then she and Olivia went back into the house through the barn. There had been no phone call from New York. Dace rang the Murray Hill house to check—but there was nothing. Harvey wasn't there, nor had he telephoned. She had scarcely expected it, she told herself that it was too soon—but too soon for what?

Harvey had had his lesson. He had gone to Scott Evans' the other night and had narrowly escaped falling into the hands of the police, who were then searching for him—if he had had any doubts on that score they had been sharply resolved. As far as he knew, the situation hadn't changed and he wasn't likely to try it again.

She left the phone and put away her coat, wondering where he was and what he was doing. Hiding in New York somewhere, in some obscure hotel or rooming house? Or would he try to get away from the city, go some place where no one knew him and he wouldn't be recognized? The thought of him doubling and dodging and fleeing in fear from a danger that no longer existed was utterly maddening. The forged check was to be obliterated, wiped out, forgotten, treated as though it had never been. Then she thought about Beecham's unexpected magnanimity. A sprat to catch a whale—in view of that other terrible charge . . . ? The dark shadow tucked away in a corner of her mind stirred; she refused to recognize its existence, averted her thoughts hastily.

Dinner was a sad meal. Madge had been crying again. Olivia was the only one who did justice to Mrs. Neibold's excellent cooking; the huge refrigerator was full of food she had prepared at the cottage and that had hardly been touched. After dinner they sat around the fire for a while, Madge sewing, Olivia playing solitaire and Dace pretending to read. At nine o'clock Gerald Straws phoned. He had no news either. They were all tired and at a little before ten they called it a day and went upstairs and to bed.

All three of them were in the south wing, Olivia next to Dace and Madge farther along in her usual room at the end. The night silence of the country in winter was profound. There were no insects, no crickets, no frogs, there wasn't even an owl. The rest of the house stretched away from them emptily, huge and untenanted and dark. Lying in bed with the curtains at the windows drawn back, Dace could see a stretch of pale sky above the woods and an up-fling of snow-covered fields off on the left; the moon was coming up. She tried to make herself easy about Harvey. After all he couldn't stay away indefinitely, the thousand dollars he had wouldn't last forever, and when he ran out of money he'd have to get in touch with someone, with her or with Joan Longstreet, or Gerald Straws or Scott Evans, and then he'd learn the truth—that all danger was over and he could come home. A hound bayed distantly, and far off in the valley a train whistle blew. It was a mournful sound in the night, lonely, forlorn. Listening for the train to whistle again, Dace fell asleep.

It was the sharp barking of a dog that woke her sometime later on. The barking was savage, persistent. It came from the direction of the outbuildings. Mr. Neibold had had a couple of hounds with him in the barn that afternoon. One of the hounds was probably barking at a fox who had come out of the woods toward the chickens, or perhaps it was a woodchuck? Then she heard something else. It was the low murmur of voices somewhere close by.

Dace got out of bed and opened her door. The light was on in the corridor and Madge and Olivia were in a huddle, their heads close together; Madge in a heavy robe over a flannel nightdress and shoes on, Olivia in a pair of Madge's pajamas, her curls rumpled and her feet bare. They both turned.

Madge said, "Oh, *dear,* Mercedes, we didn't want to wake you." The dog that was barking was one of Neibold's hounds chained in the paddock. "It's that woodchuck again after Midnight—the black silkie," Madge explained. "Midnight's broody and Neibold has her in a special nest in one of the stalls in the stable, sitting on some quail eggs. I'm going down to see, make sure the stable door is closed. I'm not sure whether I checked it before I came upstairs or not. You two girls go back to bed or you'll catch your deaths." She walked off down the corridor.

Olivia went into Dace's room with her for a cigarette. The dog kept on barking. It was a disturbing sound, at once a warning and a menace. It was cold and Dace did get back into bed. She didn't stay there. Olivia stood leaning against the window frame, smoking and looking out and talking idly. "This place is dreamy, Dace. I'm crazy about it, it's really beautiful. I hope you and Harvey will ask me up here often. . . ." Suddenly she gave an exclamation and leaned sharply forward. "*Dace*," she called in a frightened voice.

Dace threw the covers aside and joined her cousin at the window. The wing housing the dining room, the kitchen, other rooms, and finally the barn, was diagonally across from them on the far side of snow-covered lawns on which tree branches etched sharp black lines. The moon was directly overhead now. It threw brilliant light down into the snowy enclosure, silvering the front of the huge barn fully—except in one spot. The big sliding door in the middle of the barn had been rolled back. Inside in the darkness of the barn two small white circles of light were the parking lights of a car. As Olivia and Dace watched, a dark figure, a man's figure, crossed in front of the car and dissolved into blackness. Passing the lights the man was visible for less than a second, but there was no mistaking the folds of the coat he wore, a heavy tan ulster with the collar turned up. . . . The man was Harvey.

Harvey was in the car and the car was moving. Dace tugged at the window, threw it high and leaned out over the sill. "Harvey," she shouted at the top of her lungs, "Harvey." The car—it was the black and white station wagon—was some distance away from where they were, perhaps forty yards away and the motor was running. It came out of the barn fast, it was level with the dark window out of which the two girls leaned, and then it was gone, down the driveway and around the turn and there was nothing but the barking of the dog left in a landscape empty of movement.

"I don't know why you're making all this fuss, Mercedes, dear, why you're so upset—I really don't. It's foolish. You're like Elfrida, you worry too much, it'll shorten your life." Madge pulled the plug on the percolator and poured coffee into a cup and pushed it across the table to Dace. Thin sunlight flooded through the windows. It was half past eight. The three women were breakfasting in the kitchen.

Dace took a sip of the scalding liquid and lit a cigarette. "I'm worrying," she said, "because now that Harvey has a car he can go anywhere he likes, fast and far. He won't bother calling anyone up, and if he doesn't call how is he going to find out that—that the police are no longer interested in him?"

Madge stirred sugar into her own coffee. She said meditatively, "If I know Harvey, he'll get tired of wandering around alone. He was never one to like being by himself for long, for any length of time. He always wanted company—and besides, he'll know you're worried, Dace. But there is one thing you could do. You could call the police and tell them that Harvey has the station wagon and have them flag it down."

Olivia stopped attacking her bacon and eggs with appetite. "It's an idea, Dace. . . . Maybe that would be best. . . ." But she was doubtful.

Dace wasn't in the least doubtful. As long as Harvey didn't know the truth, if he still thought he was wanted for forgery, there was a strong likelihood, or at least a distinct possibility, that he would do something desperate if the police tried to take him by force. Anything could happen before they had a chance to explain. She could still hear the shot that had been fired in the darkness and the snow when Scott Evans tried to run away from the police down there on University Place in New York. "No," she said, "we can't tell the police, we've had enough of them, we'll just have to wait, that's all. Do you think Mr. Neibold is suspicious, Madge? That wasn't a very good story we told him, and he doesn't look like a stupid man."

When Madge had gone downstairs last night to see if the black hen was all right, she couldn't get into the barn from the house. The door there was fast. The big wooden bolt on the other side, the barn side, had been dropped into its socket. It had made Madge suspicious and she had gone straight to the phone and had called Neibold before she knew anything about Harvey. Neibold had come dashing over from his cottage. He had gone first into the barn. No one was there, but neither was the station wagon. By that time Madge knew it was Harvey who had driven off in it and she had told Neibold that it was all right, that Mrs. Allert had lent it to a friend who had dropped in late and that she didn't know this when she rang him.

The story was wretchedly thin. It was true that the big barn door wasn't locked and anybody could take the car

110

keys from the keyboard against a wall, all neatly labeled, but if a visitor had come to the house on foot late in the evening, which was in itself unlikely, why didn't whoever it was provide himself with a means of transportation or stay the night? This wasn't New York where you could whistle up a cab at any hour.

Madge said she was sure that there was no danger where Tom Neibold was concerned. He was close-mouthed, a real Yankee, and he didn't babble, and no matter what he might think himself he wouldn't do any loose talking.

They left it at that. For the rest Harvey's own movements were clear enough. At some time during the evening, after dark anyhow, he had come to the farm. There were plenty of ways he could have got there; by bus, which would drop him a quarter of a mile away to the east, or by train, no more than three-quarters of a mile down the valley. There was another possibility. Thinking of it Dace went cold inwardly.

Suppose Harvey had been on the farm some time. He knew it inside and out, and there were plenty of places in which he could have concealed himself, sheltering at night in the stables or in the huge barn loft, and by day there were the pine woods. Behind their thick green walls he could have kept the house under observation. And she and Hugh Clavering had been at the edge of the woods when Hugh had made that plea to her. . . . If Harvey was there he could have heard. . . . She recalled her own shocked feeling of being under observation when snow slid from the branches around the turn of the path. It was Gerald Straws who had appeared, but Harvey could have been under the trees in the brown gloom of the wood. . . .

She finished her coffee and lit another cigarette. There was no use worrying about what might have happened. It mightn't be so at all. The thing now was to do something constructive.

Gerald had a car and it was possible that he might pick up Harvey's trail. The black and white station wagon, if not unusual, was at least identifiable. According to Mr. Neibold—Madge had asked him—the tank of the station wagon was only about a quarter full. Harvey would have to stop somewhere for more gas within a certain number

111

of miles. She explained this and both Madge and Olivia thought it was a good idea to get hold of Gerald and have him follow it up.

Dace went to the phone and called long distance. It was only a little after nine but he wasn't in his apartment. She called the investment house where he worked, as he complained sadly, for a pittance. He wasn't there either.

Dace abandoned the phone. Madge was leaving the farm herself that day and Olivia had to get back to town. Less than half an hour later the two girls were on board a train for New York.

TEN

Dace and Olivia reached Grand Central at eleven-fifty and parted there. Olivia went home to her own apartment on the subway, to get fresh clothes and do all the things she had to do to get ready for the remainder of the week at the office. Dace walked down to the Murray Hill house in the teeth of a shrewd wind through banks of dirty snow piled high against building fronts and in the gutters. When she got into the welcome warmth of the house there was no news, but she didn't expect any. Harvey hadn't taken—you couldn't say stolen because it was now his own—the black and white station wagon from the farm for the purpose of driving to New York in it. What he evidently meant to do was to take refuge in distance, sit it out somewhere far away for a while, under the delusion that the police were still looking for him.

Fear was the spur, fear of disgrace, of exposure, to his friends, his business associates, his host of acquaintances, his entire world. "Did you hear the news? Harvey Allert's in jail. *No!* Yes—he's been arrested, for forgery." This sort of thing would ring in his ears. His agony, baseless agony, had to be brought to an end.

113

The first thing to do was to get hold of Gerald Straws. She called Gerald's office but he still wasn't there and his secretary didn't know where he could be located. It was then after twelve and Dace decided that he was probably out to lunch. He oughtn't to be long. She gave her phone number and asked the girl to have him call her as soon as he got in, hung up and went into the living room. She found the road map she wanted in one of the big desk drawers—Harvey had maps of practically every inch of the continent—and settled down to study it.

The gas in the station-wagon tank, three to four gallons of it, wouldn't at best take him more than sixty miles, and he would hardly let it get that low if he could help it—so say fifty miles before he would have to get more. With a red pencil she drew a ring on the map with the farm as a center. It might be difficult to find the service station where he had stopped in order to fill the tank, but it was not impossible. He would probably take one of the main highways in whatever direction he was moving, and there weren't too many of them.

Gerald didn't call her until almost two o'clock and by then, valuable time was being lost, she was chafing at the bit. She told him quickly about the station wagon and what had happened the night before, and explained her plan. She said that if they could pick Harvey up at one given spot they'd have some sort of idea of where he was heading. His description, plus the black and white station wagon and the license number, would be identification enough. There couldn't be too many all-night gas stations in that part of the country—he might even have had to pull up and wait until morning.

Gerald was a douche of cold water. He agreed with her about the wisdom of not calling in the police. They'd done quite enough harm as it was, and if Harvey was suddenly confronted by them with an order to stop, he might easily lose his head and do something hairbrained. Gerald didn't agree with her about the chances of locating him. He said there were a vast number of side roads, lots of them with gas pumps, and if and when they did manage to find the right one it would be too late; by then Harvey would be hundreds of miles away. There might have been a chance

114

if they had gone after him last night; now there was little or none. In any case he himself was tied up and would be for the next couple of hours. He said he'd see her later on in the day.

Dace, surprised and shocked by Gerald's reaction, was too angry to say any more than "Don't bother, I may not be here," icily. She left the telephone in a cold fury. Gerald Straws was Harvey's oldest and closest friend, yet he didn't seem to care, or even to be particularly interested in Harvey's flight from a threat that no longer existed but which to him was nonetheless real. If you wanted to get a thing done, the best way was to do it yourself. There was no reason in the world why she shouldn't get the Benz and start out on Harvey's trail, none whatever. She mightn't succeed but she could at least try, and anything was better than sitting around doing nothing.

She went upstairs and changed quickly into another suit and flats, planning as she dressed. She would go as far as she could that day, stay at a hotel overnight and continue searching tomorrow. It was only twenty past two and if she stepped on it she could make Poughkeepsie not very long after dark. It was lucky that she had money. She had gone to the bank before starting for the farm and drawn out a hundred and twenty-five of the two hundred and eight that was there. A hundred of it had been meant for the maids, but they would have to wait.

She phoned the garage and asked them to deliver the Benz, then rang for Gertrude and told her that she might or might not be in to dinner. The less the girl knew, the better. Twenty minutes later she was behind the wheel of the Benz heading west for the Highway when she thought suddenly of Olivia. She should have let Olivia know. . . . She put her foot on the brake and took it off again. It would be just as easy to phone from a drug store and would take less time than to go back to the house.

She found two drug stores with no parking space, she located a third and pulled up. Both booths were occupied with what looked like interminable talkers. The minutes were flying. Exasperation bit into her and she turned on her heel. The best thing to do was to stop at Olivia's apartment, which was on East Fourth Street; it wouldn't lose her more than a quarter of an hour. She could get onto the Highway at Eighteenth.

She drove east to Fifth, and down Fifth and then west around Washington Square, deep in snow under the leafless trees. Another maddening search for a parking space; New York was getting impossible. She finally got space down the block from Olivia's when a man pulled out. Olivia's apartment building, a big, newish rabbit warren, was on the south side of the street. Just as Dace was veering to cross the street, a man ducked back into a doorway twenty feet out in front of her. The suddenness of the movement attracted her attention. As she came level with the doorway she turned her head. The man standing in the doorway in shadow was Gerald Straws.

Dace pulled up. "Gerald—what are you doing in this neighborhood?" Surprise made the demand sound abrupt, and she was still angry with him.

Gerald finished lighting his pipe calmly and stepped out on the sidewalk. He wasn't a bit ruffled, and he ignored her coolness. "I had to see a man"—he gestured at the building behind him—"but he's not in, worse luck, although he said he would be. What are *you* doing here, Dace?"

"I want to see Olivia. She lives over there in Thirty-eight."

"Oh—that's right. I have to wait around anyhow, I'll go along with you."

Dace was genuinely puzzled. Gerald had told her over the phone a little while ago that he'd be tied up for a couple of hours, and he was alone. Rather peculiar that the man he wanted to see lived directly across the street from Olivia, a man who wasn't there—but Gerald must be telling the truth, because why on earth should he be watching Olivia's apartment? She couldn't make head or tail of it.

Number Thirty-eight was a walk-up. They mounted two flights of stairs together, Gerald asking questions about the night before at the farm, Dace answering absently. Perhaps Olivia wasn't home and Gerald had been waiting for her, but if that was the case why didn't he say so?

116

Olivia was home. She came to the door at once, pulling it open quickly as soon as the bell rang.

Whoever Olivia had expected to see it wasn't Gerald or her, Dace thought—she was startled, brought up short, and stood staring at them. A fraction of a second of blankness—then she exclaimed, smiling welcomingly, "Dace, Gerald—come in." Her smile went. "Has something happened?" she asked anxiously. "Have you heard . . . ?"

Dace shook her head. They shouldn't, she decided, have come barging in like this on Olivia—she had her own life to live. She was a reticent girl and always had been, she did little or no talking about her own private concern. She was probably expecting some man. A ribbon held her freshly washed curls in place and the housecoat she wore was a very pretty one. She looked lovely, like a ripe peach with her tawny skin and the glow in her cheeks. In the small square hall Dace said no, she wouldn't take her coat off, she was only going to stay a minute. She was starting to explain what she intended to do when the doorbell rang again. Olivia went to the door and opened it, and stared. The man who came in was Hugh.

"Hugh Clavering . . ." Olivia was as surprised as Dace to see Hugh there. Hugh explained quickly. He had followed Dace's car away from the Murray Hill house in a cab, had lost her and then had decided to try here on a chance. He had just come from a meeting with Beecham. Late last night Harvey had got a ticket for speeding on the Black Rock Turnpike north of Bedford. The ticket hadn't come to light until around noon that day. The state policeman who gave it to him thought nothing of it—it was simply routine, the order to pick up Harvey had already been rescinded—but McKee had been notified and McKee had informed Beecham.

Dace was dismayed. The police knew Harvey had the black and white station wagon. . . . It was the very thing she had wanted to avoid. She said, "Are they going to . . . . ? Will they . . . ?"

Hugh shook his head. "No, they're not interested any longer, but I knew you were worried and that you'd want to know."

He stayed only a minute. He was already late for an appointment uptown. His manner was crisp, and pleasant. There was no private glance at Dace, no unspoken communication between them. Hugh had washed the slate clean up there at the farm when she gave him her answer, just as he had washed it clean four years ago. . . .

She crushed the small ache inside her with a touch of fierceness. It was better this way. Hugh was sensible and decisive, not a man to moon and dream and lose himself in the abstractions of an inner world that was impossible of attainment. Now that she had put herself out of the picture, there would be another woman—there were always women with Hugh, that was the rock they had originally crashed on. Three strikes—and out. She had forgiven him twice, and accepted what he said, laughing at her inexperience, otherworldliness. "Dace, you're a child, it means nothing, nothing whatever, you're the only real one." But the third time had been one too many for her pride—and perhaps her vanity. That was what Hugh had told her, storming at her. He was probably right. It no longer mattered. It was over. The room seemed peculiarly empty when he left.

Olivia went away to telephone and Dace took off her coat and sat down. Some of the urgency had gone out of her proposed journey in search of Harvey but he still had to be found, even if there was no longer any danger from the police. Gerald was wandering around the room looking at things, some of them from the Murray Hill house; the Degas Harvey had given Olivia when she fell in love with it, the little row of ivory figurines. Olivia came back and Dace told the two of them what she meant to do. Olivia thought it sounded like a good idea. "I wish I could go with you but I thought Gerald . . ."

Gerald interrupted her, speaking with more force than he usually exerted. "Dace, my child, you're crazy. *You* go looking for Harvey?" He smiled. "You wouldn't get to first base. A wife pursuing a fleeing husband spells trouble in any language—don't you know that? You'd get absolutely no information, not an iota, not a scrap."

Olivia didn't agree with him. She still thought it a good idea. Gerald said, eyeing her, "Do you propose joining Dace on this—expedition?"

"I can't," Olivia said. "I've got to be in the office tomorrow, but I wish I could."

"You do, do you?"

There was something going on between the two of them, a sort of tug of war of some kind. . . . A sudden thought struck Dace out of the blue. Harvey was very fond of Olivia—pictures flashed through her mind, of Harvey's picking Olivia up in his arms and waltzing her around the living room over her laughing protests—"Stick to me kid and you'll wear diamonds"; of his holding her off out at the dock at Southampton and saying, "Isn't she sweet, isn't she luscious and good enough to eat?" Could Harvey have phoned Olivia and sworn her to secrecy? Could he be coming here? And could Gerald have found out about it somehow or other, or got an inkling of it, and was that why he had been down there across the street watching Olivia's apartment?'

The idea fell apart almost before it was fully formed. Jim Bates, the man who had asked Olivia out the other night, the night of the bitter fiasco on University Place, arrived. Bates was the man Olivia had been expecting. She dimpled and smiled and her whole face lit up when he came in. Introductions, polite nothings, they couldn't talk with Mr. Bates there; five minutes later Gerald and Dace were out in the street.

Once they were alone together Gerald's manner changed. The narrow attention went out of him and he became himself again, cool and thoughtful and more than a little detached. Was he in love with Olivia? Dace wondered. Could he be? He had never given any sign of it, but then perhaps he wouldn't. . . . He was an odd man. Her faith in him, in his reliability, had been badly shaken earlier in the day.

Over a beer in a neighboring bar they had it out about Harvey and the station wagon, and Gerald finally persuaded Dace to go home. He'd take over the search himself. He didn't think too much of his chances but in any case they were better than hers. Harvey had a seventeen-hour start but he had to eat and he had to sleep, which would cut his lead. Gerald took down the license number of the station wagon and then said he'd better get going, enough time had elapsed as it was. Outside in the street he hailed a cab. Dace went back to the Benz and drove north to the Murray Hill house, if not in a happier at least in a more hopeful mood than she had been in since Harvey had walked off almost a week ago. It was a week that seemed like half a lifetime. That was on Wednesday afternoon.

ELEVEN

At seven-thirty on the night of Thursday, January the sixteenth, a Mr. Harold Allen arrived at the Hotel Charles in Danbury, Connecticut, picked up his reservation made by telephone the day before, and registered. As was usual at that hour the lobby of the hotel was jammed. The Charles did a terrific trade. Built in the late twenties, a grandiose and towering structure standing in its own grounds, it was ahead of its time and had teetered on the brink of failure for years, until conventions began to come along. After that it was clear sailing. The Charles became known for its handling of conventions and they had more than saved its bacon. The hotel was always crowded and noisy with a lot going on; the dining room was good, and it had two name bands and an excellent floor show.

When Mr. Allen got there he had to forge a way to the desk through the crowd besieging it. The three harassed clerks were up to their ears in demands and complaints and general clamor and din. Allen was a tall man in an expensive light tan ulster with a hat pulled down over his eyes. The clerk who handled him gave him scarcely a glance. Half a dozen other people were demanding his attention, vociferously. One in particular, a small, cocky woman, kept clacking at him. Allen's reservation was in the proper pigeonhole and everything was in order. Allen duly registered, the clerk shoved the key of a single with bath on the eleventh floor across the desk and rang the bell for a boy. The man in the light tan coat picked up his pigskin bag with his initials on it in gold, turned away and was swallowed up in the crowd.

Noise, confusion, music, voices, people in knots, people streaming around the knots coming and going, from the elevators, the dining room, the cocktail lounges. No one noticed Mr. Harold Allen. There were two conventions in full blast and the participants were busy with their own affairs. A maharajah could have ridden to and fro on an elephant, if he could have found the room, without provoking a glance.

There was one exception to this general eyelessness and it had to do, not with Mr. Harold Allen but with a young woman in a red coat fastened at the sleeves and down the front with pearl buttons as big as saucers. The young woman's blond head was bare and she was carrying a mink scarf over one arm. There were two fauteuils at either end of the lobby. A Mrs. Christianberry was seated on the one at the north end waiting for her husband, who was having a shave in the barber shop, and enjoying the sights. The girl in the red coat attracted Mrs. Christianberry's attention, or rather the coat did. She loved it, particularly the buttons, and thought it would look well on her daughter May.

The girl who wore the coat was also waiting for someone. She stood facing Mrs. Christianberry, smoking a cigarette near a pillar a short distance away. All at once she took a step and her face lit up. She was speaking to a tall man in a light tan coat, shaking hands with him.

The man's back was turned and Mrs. Christianberry couldn't see his face. After a moment he put his arm through the girl's and the two of them walked off in the general direction of the elevators and Mrs. Christianberry lost sight of them in an engulfing army of laughing, talking men and women wearing badges and making their way to the dining room. That was at twenty minutes of eight.

At five of eight a Mr. Peter Swanson walked into the lobby of the Charles and made his way as fast as possible toward the cocktail lounge. He was to meet Floss Crosby there for drinks and dinner and he was already twenty-five minutes late, which wasn't bad for him, he reflected cheerfully. He looked around. Floss was nowhere in sight. She wasn't inside the lounge or near the entrance to it. Swanson went into the bar, parked himself on a stool from which he could see the door, ordered a Scotch on the rocks, lit a cigarette and made himself comfortable.

Floss, he decided with a grin, was giving him a dose of his own medicine, she'd come along in a few minutes. Floss didn't come along. It got to be ten after eight and then twenty after, and Swanson began to seethe. A joke was a joke but if she was going to stand him up in earnest she might at least have had the decency to give him a ring and say so, or if she had been held up and couldn't help it she could have him paged. She was the one who suggested coming here, for lobster and Trotter's band. Where the hell was she? In all the time he had known her she had never pulled a trick like this before. He got madder by the minute. At a quarter of nine Mr. Peter Swanson stalked out of the cocktail lounge and the hotel in a red rage.

The body wasn't discovered until the next morning.

Two chambermaids coming to work at a little before half past six almost fell into the shallow pit in which the shocking figure lay face down in the snow where it had broken through the icy crust. The maids hurried off and gave the alarm, quietly, and less than half an hour later the Danbury police were on the scene. The ranking officer was Captain Durkin. At shortly after nine A.M. Durkin called Inspector McKee in New York, he knew the Scotsman and had worked on cases with him before.

Durkin said, "Maybe there's nothing in it for you and you won't be interested, Inspector, but I remembered the name—kind of an odd one—and I thought you'd like to know," and told McKee. A Mr. Harvey Allert had been paged at the Hotel Charles there in Danbury the night before. There was no Harvey Allert registered as a guest at the hotel but there was a Mr. Harold Allen, and it was from the window of Allen's room on the eleventh floor that a Miss Floss Crosby had plunged to her death the previous night.

McKee and Captain Pierson of his own squad arrived at the Hotel Charles some two hours later. Durkin was waiting for them and he led the way into an office that had been put at their disposal by the manager, Mr. Trask. Mr. Trask, plump, brisk and well-tailored, was affable and anxious to help. He was not at all cast down by the tragedy that had taken place in the hotel under his charge. It was an awful thing, of course, and they didn't like it, but as far as casting a shadow on the hotel went, times had changed. Things were altogether different nowadays; instead of avoiding room 1105 people would be lined up clamoring for it.

Durkin and the Danbury police had been busy, and a good deal had already been established. The dead girl was a Miss Floss Crosby, a fashion model for one of the big specialty shops in town. She lived with a friend, a divorcée named Olga Peters, in an apartment on Leroy Street near the center of the city. Mrs. Peters had already been interviewed. Floss Crosby had only been in Danbury three months; she had come originally from New York where Mrs. Peters had also formerly worked and where they had become acquainted a year or so ago; they were both in the same line.

Mrs. Peters couldn't tell them very much about the dead girl except that Floss was lively and smart and good company and that she went about a lot. The current man—she was neither married nor engaged and he was just a friend—was a Mr. Peter Swanson. Floss had had a date with Swanson last night for dinner and dancing at the Charles. Peter Swanson had also been interviewed, a frightened and pallid Swanson, at the department store where he worked in the credit office.

As far as Floss Crosby's past went Swanson could tell them even less than Mrs. Peters. He had met the girl at a party in late October and they had been going around together maybe a couple of times a week since that. There was nothing serious to it, they were just good friends. Swanson described his own movements the night before, his date with Floss Crosby at the Charles for drinks and dinner, and Floss's nonappearance. He was late, he admitted he generally was, and at first he thought Floss was giving him a lesson so he waited patiently. But she didn't come. He swore that he had been in the cocktail lounge where they were to have met, from about five

124

minutes of eight until a quarter of nine, at which time he left the hotel, had a hamburger in a dog wagon on Grant Street, and then went home to his hotel room.

So far the Danbury men hadn't been able to find out just when the dead girl had arrived at the Charles, but the overnight guests had been questioned and a Mrs. Christianberry, waiting in the lobby for her husband to join her, remembered Floss Crosby's red coat and then the girl herself, and the girl's meeting with a tall man in a light tan coat carrying a pale tan leather bag, an expensive-looking bag, at shortly after half past seven.

Durkin's findings on the man who had registered as Harold Allen, and to whom room 1105 had been assigned, were scant to say the least. The desk clerk had only the vaguest memory of Allen, which was not only understandable but, in view of the conditions that prevailed, almost inevitable. The elevator operators had no memory of Allen at all, nor had there been any providential chambermaids hanging about when Allen and the girl rode up to the eleventh floor. From the time Mrs. Christianberry saw Floss Crosby walk off in the direction of the elevators with him, no one had laid eyes on Mr. Harold Allen, coming or going.

They had established Floss Crosby's having been in room 1105 only by a stroke of luck. Unnoticed, a button had been torn off her coat in her useless struggle with her killer. Providentially the button had rolled under the radiator and out of sight. Because there was nothing else to show that either Allen or the girl had been in the room at all, such fingerprints as there were had been checked first thing but they belonged to the cleaning staff.

The autopsy hadn't yet been done and the time of death was uncertain, but Danbury's medical examiner said positively that in his opinion the girl had been murdered. The marks on her throat indicated clearly that she had been choked, more than probably with a white silk scarf she wore around her neck under her coat. The scarf had been found lying in the snow some distance from the body, and had probably been thrown out after she was sent through the window so that there should be nothing left to identify the room she had been in. McKee, Pierson and Captain Durkin went upstairs.

125

Room 1105 was the usual hotel bedroom, a little flossy, a little too bright—but then the Charles was not now an upper-bracket hostelry. Not, McKee reflected, at all the sort of place Harvey Allert, if Allen was Allert, would ordinarily be found in—which could have been the reason why he had chosen it. His tenure of office had been short, the soap in the bathroom was still unwrapped and the bed hadn't been slept in. The killing had probably taken place without any loss of time. Little or no imagination was required to reset the scene. Floss Crosby and the man who called himself Allen had walked in in amity. An easy "Sit down, Floss, make yourself comfortable," perhaps "Let's have a drink," and then a quick pounce from behind and the silk scarf seized and made into a rope. It was dark outside then. The window was wide and faced north and the girl was smallish and slight. If she wasn't dead when she was sent through the window the fall would have killed her. The man down on the register as Allen had taken no chances.

Before leaving New York McKee had got samples of Harvey Allert's handwriting from the district attorney's office. He also had an enlargement of the snapshot of Allert that they had removed from the Murray Hill house with Mercedes Allert's consent. Shown the photograph, the clerk who had processed Mr. Harold Allen was a broken reed. He said, "That's him," positively, and then be hedged. Maybe it was—but he couldn't be dead sure, he couldn't swear to it.

McKee and Pierson studied the card that bore Mr. Harold Allen's registration, his name and simply the address New York. There was no similarity between the two specimens, but the very difference between them could be suspicious—it would have to wait on the experts.

The telephone call asking the hotel to have Mr. Harvey Allert brought to the phone had come through at around nine-fifteen. The rushed operator thought it was a woman who had called but she couldn't be positive. She had checked her list of guests and had informed the caller that there was no Mr. Harvey Allert staying as a guest at the Charles, and that was that. The huge car park back of the hotel was equally barren of results, it offered no clue to the black and white station wagon in which Harvey Allert had driven off from the Duchess County farm on the previous Tuesday night. After a word with the manager and a look at the parking lot, McKee gave up hope. The lot had been dark and busy. There were only a couple of attendants, and the guests parked at their own risk.

Pierson, McKee and Durkin discussed the situation over sandwiches and a beer in the office that had been placed at their disposal. Harvey Allert—Harold Allen, to match the initials on the pigskin bag Mrs. Allert said her husband had taken with him when he left the Murray Hill house a week earlier. It leaped to the eye. No other conclusion seemed possible; anything else would have been too much of a coincidence. But there were a number of questions to be answered. First and foremost, if Allen was Allert, why had he come here to this big, noisy Danbury hotel?

You could answer that by saying that Allert, knowing nothing of the fact that the warrant against him had been quashed, was tired of being on the run and that it was as good a place to hide out as any. He could have had his meals served in his room and lain low here indefinitely. But the telephone call asking to have Mr. Harvey Allert paged didn't jibe with this—unless someone had seen and recognized him in the lobby and had called from the hotel itself, or from somewhere close by. Either that or someone had got on his trail somehow, his wife or one of his relatives or friends searching for him. There could be a third explanation. Allert himself might have told someone he could be reached at the hotel the night before.

And then there was the actual killing itself. Only a madman killed without a motive. Was Beecham's contention that Harvey Allert had engineered his stepmother's death true? Was Miss Floss Crosby the missing piece of the puzzle that had already been looked for in vain? Did Floss Crosby know something, had she seen something—perhaps without being aware of it—that would be lethal to Allert, something that would prove his guilt in bringing about his stepmother's fatal crash? The girl herself and her history would have to be looked into thoroughly. . . . At the moment there was nothing more for them in the hotel itself. Leaving Pierson behind him to coöperate with Captain Durkin on the spot, McKee hopped a local plane from Boston and went back to New York. He was in his office an hour and a half later. He didn't stay there. The Commissioner wanted to see him. McKee grunted and went downtown.

"I *told* you so, Inspector. I warned you—right here in this room. But you wouldn't listen. Harvey Allert killed Elfrida as surely as if he took an axe to her, and this Crosby girl found out about it, or put two and two together, so *she* was washed out."

Beecham and John Francis Dwyer, New York's district attorney, were with the Commissioner. It was only ten minutes past three and the lights were on but the big room was dim, with patches of shadow in the corners. An icy fog pressed up against the windows. Out on the rivers whistles blew and horns bellowed mournfully.

Beecham sat heavily upright in his chair, a monolithic figure of triumph, massive and accusing. The Scotsman said dryly, "There was nothing to listen to, then. You saw the report on Elfrida Allert's car."

Beecham threw the report aside. "Bah. Stuff and nonsense—a Scotch verdict—not proven. You've got your proof now, and plenty of it. If Harvey Allert isn't guilty, why did he kill that girl up there in that Danbury hotel?"

Both Carey and Dwyer were in agreement with Beecham, but McKee was not going to permit himself to be rushed. He resented having been called down here and away from work that had to be done fast. It was a waste of valuable time.

He said, "Counselor, your conviction, or mine, that a man is guilty is about as useful as a handful of straw unless it's backed up with facts. It's got to be proved that Allen and Allert are one and the same man, it's got to be proved also that Allert had exclusive opportunity, that someone else didn't follow Allen and the girl up there to the eleventh floor, someone who's hiding behind Allert, playing him for a patsy, a fall guy, a . . ."

Beecham threw himself back in his chair, his big white face tinged with a delicate purple. "Come off it, Inspector. Harvey Allert's as guilty as hell, and you know it. You've got your killer all right. What are you going to do about it? That's what I want to know—what are you going to do?"

Lighting a cigarette and blowing smoke McKee remained calm. "Exception, Counselor. Not my bureau's killer. This is not our case, it's Connecticut's."

He went on to say that they would work on it, of course—Harvey Allert and the girl whose broken body had landed in the snow up there under the window of the room on the eleventh floor of the Hotel Charles in Danbury occupied by Allen-Allert, were both New Yorkers. The most pressing, most immediate task was to get hold of Harvey Allert. If he was still driving the black and white station wagon, it would be a comparatively simple matter. If he had got rid of the car, the time and the place where he ditched it might provide a lead. Meanwhile Floss Crosby's connection with Harvey Allert had to be established more firmly. His wife, Mercedes Allert, might know, or the Longstreets, or Scott Evans or Gerald Straws—if they'd talk.

"Do they know about this murder of the Crosby girl up there in Danbury?" Dwyer asked.

"Not from me or from any of my staff, they don't," McKee said. "And Durkin's playing dumb on the Harvey Allert angle—if we want to get our hands on Allert the less publicity at this stage the better." He added slowly, "But I'm not at all sure that they oughtn't to be told—or at least that Mrs. Allert shouldn't."

"Why?" Dwyer demanded.

"Because if she doesn't know she may get into real trouble. A man who's killed twice isn't going to hesitate about a third time. If her husband should manage to get in touch with her without our knowing about it, and if she should let him see that she has any suspicions about his implication in his stepmother's death, then—well, it mightn't be too healthy for her. Everything else aside and even under normal conditions, he doesn't seem to be the most stable of characters."

There Beecham was in complete agreement with him. There was no telling what Harvey Allert would do, ever. After a little more talk, and chafing at the delay, McKee said he had work to do and finally managed to make his escape. On his way out of the building he ran into New York's chief medical examiner and his own personal friend, Fernandez.

Fernandez was mounting the outer steps jauntily, swinging a cane, very elegant in a dark overcoat with a white silk scarf at the throat, looking like deposed royalty in not very much of a disguise. He brought the cane up in a smart salute.

"Whither away fair Lydia—I hear you're up to your eyeballs in our more elite circles, Chris. You don't look good."

They chatted for a moment and then McKee described Harvey Allert. "I've never laid eyes on the man but from what I've heard from his wife and his relatives and friends . . ." He said that Allert was a man of thirty-nine, high-strung, given to moods, erratic and an egotist, on top of the world one minute, in the depths the next, by turns sullen and withdrawn or wildly exuberant.

"Umm . . ." Fernandez considered. "It's hard to say offhand but he sounds like a rather clear-cut manic-depressive. . . . Of course, I'd have to see him."

"Would you say a suicidal type?"

"On impulse, very definitely yes."

"Dangerous to others?"

"It's hard to say but in the manic phase, if he were cornered, yes."

Harvey Allert had been cornered twice. He had been cornered by his stepmother, who stood solidly in the way of an inheritance he badly needed and felt should be his own, and he had been cornered in some fashion or other by Floss Crosby up there in the Hotel Charles in Danbury when he was running away from the police. Both women were dead.

McKee parted from Fernandez and returned to the office. Before going downtown he had set the wheels in motion and the hunt was on for the black and white station wagon with or without Harvey Allert at the wheel. Men had been sent to talk to the Longstreets, Scott Evans, Gerald Straws and Mercedes Allert. The Longstreets had never heard of any woman named Floss Crosby. Neither Scott Evans nor Gerald Straws had been located, and the latter had been away from his office for two days. Very interesting this last.

McKee went on thinking. Harvey Allert's whole procedure had a smell of collusion about it, or at least the strong possibility of such collusion, as though someone in the know, on scene, was keeping Allert wise as to what was going on and what was being done generally. He could be wrong. He had given no intensive thought to the case and, as in any given case, you had to live with it for a while to get the touch, the feel of it. . . .

There was no report in on Mrs. Allert. And then there was. McKee was only back at his desk a few minutes when the outside phone rang. It was Bronstein, the first-grade detective who had gone to talk to Mercedes Allert.

Mrs. Allert wasn't in the house in the court on Murray Hill. No one was. The house was dark and silent.

Bronstein was phoning from a drug store on the corner of Lex and Thirty-sixth. "I knocked and I rang, back and front, and there was no answer, nothing doing, not a sound and not a light on. Want I should go back to the house and stick around and wait for her, Inspector, in case she comes home?" he asked.

McKee didn't answer for a moment. His gaze was narrow and fixed on the fog pushing up against the window beyond his desk in the fading purple light. It would soon be night. Then he said to Bronstein, "Go back to the house and stay there, I'll come round."

TWELVE

The black and white station wagon that the police of seven states, but particularly the police of Connecticut and New York, were so anxious to get their hands on had already been found, but not by anyone connected with the law. Mr. and Mrs. Neibold, the farmer and his wife who managed the Allert estate in Duchess County, were leaving that afternoon on their yearly vacation of two weeks in Miami. They were to start at three and stop over in New York that night.

At around two o'clock that day, their packing finished, Tom Neibold took the jeep and made a swing around the estate for a last check, to see that everything was shipshape and in order. There wasn't much to do at that time of the year and what little stock there was would be taken care of by Jorden, Mrs. Neibold's brother, but Jorden wasn't the brightest lad in the world. Neibold checked the outbuildings, the stable, the barn and the house itself, long and white and melancholy in the fog that lay over the whole countryside and that, if he knew his onions, would soon turn to sleet. The doors and windows of the house were all tight.

Getting back into the jeep Neibold put the house behind him and swung into the snow-covered lane that ran downhill through the fir plantation to the south gate. The old barn in the back pasture near the gate was due to come down in the spring. But it was in pretty bad shape and maybe Jorden ought to start work on it while they were away, he could get plenty of help during the winter. Better take a look at it while he was over here. He rounded a turn and pulled up in front of the old barn. Once it had stood in the open but now it was surrounded by trees on three sides. The big doors facing the lane were fastened simply with a wooden hasp. Neibold lifted the hasp, pulled open one of the big doors crooked in its frame, and stood still, staring.

The station wagon that had been taken by one of young Mrs. Allert's friends last Tuesday night after the funeral was there looming up solidly in the gloom.

Neibold massaged his chin and went on staring at the car. He was as puzzled as he was surprised. Why put the station wagon here where no one would ever think of looking for it, instead of returning it to him and letting him put it in its proper place? It could stand in this old shed for months and no one would know where it was. It was a fool thing to do, it didn't make sense, Neibold couldn't understand it at all. He stopped shaving his chin, went into the barn and gave the station wagon a good going over.

It was undamaged, the fenders intact and no scratches or dents, and it had stood there for some time, a good many hours anyhow; the radiator was stone cold. The keys weren't in the ignition or anywhere inside the car that he could find, so he couldn't drive it back and put it where it belonged. It would have to stay where it was for the time being. Miss Madge had a spare set of keys. She could send them to Jorden and Jorden could take care of it; he could be trusted to do that. Neibold closed the doors, dropped the hasp into place with a worried feeling, retraced his steps to the jeep and looked down the lane.

The big wooden gate a hundred yards downhill was closed, but that was the way the station wagon had been driven in, over the back road. Better get in touch with Miss Madge right off—Neibold drove home and called her at her niece's in Vermont.

That was at twenty minutes of three. Madge Tarbel called Dace at a quarter of.

Dace was alone in the Murray Hill house when the

phone rang; she had given the maids the whole week end off, glad to be rid of Gertrude and her inquisitive eyes. She got out of her chair in the living room and went to answer the phone lethargically. She had about given up hope of locating Harvey through the station wagon. Gerald Straws had been in touch with her from time to time. Gerald had been right and she had been wrong, the scent was cold, too cold to follow, he had had no success whatever.

He wasn't the only one looking for Harvey. Kermit Longstreet had taken a hand, and so had Hugh. Hugh had called her up after he left Olivia's the other day. She had been surprised and touched by his offer to help in the search for Harvey. He had been brisk and almost formal about it, he had made no effort to push aside the barrier she had erected between them. He spoke as a friend, nothing more. "You're worried and I've got a car, and your husband ought to be found—as fast as possible."

Neither Hugh nor Gerald, nor Kermit Longstreet, had been able to pick up so much as a whisper of the station wagon. It was hopeless. Harvey would return when it suited him and not before. Meanwhile there was nothing to do but wait and wait and wait through the endless dragging hours, haunted and besieged and stabbed at by that dreadful accusation of Beecham's about Harvey and Elfrida's car. She had fought it off, had turned her back on it, and then had finally faced the horror. There was only one way to annihilate it—and that was to ask Harvey, straight out. She would know then. She always knew when Harvey was lying. His voice, his face, the look in his eyes, the very air around him shouted it aloud. But she couldn't ask him when he wasn't there. . . .

Out in the hall she dropped into the little gilt chair and picked up the instrument with a languid hand. It was Madge calling from Vermont, and Madge gave her the information that had just been given to her by Tom Neibold.

At Madge's first words Dace sat up with a sharp movement. Blood was flowing through her veins again strongly, vigorously. Now there was hope, now things would settle themselves, and the long nightmare would be over. Harvey was, he must be, at the farm. What better

134

place could he find where he could keep under cover safely, with practically no risk of being discovered, with a roof over his head and plenty of food, the cupboards stacked, hams and flitches of bacon in the cellar, and the Deep-Freeze loaded with fresh vegetables from the garden, so that he wouldn't have to appear in public at all? Why hadn't they thought of it before? The house was a perfect shelter. It was invisible from the road, the Neibold's cottage was almost half a mile off to the south . . . .

Madge went on talking. She was puzzled and a little worried. "I don't understand it, Dace. Why didn't Harvey put the car back in the barn, the right one? Why did he put it in that old thing where no one would ever think of looking for it? Oh well," she added philosophically, "it's his own and he can do as he likes, but it does seem—queer." She had told Neibold to leave the car where it was and go on with his vacation as planned, but . . .

Dace thought swiftly. Energy and force were back in her, and her brain was working again. Harvey at the farm . . . He was unpredictable, he might suddenly decide to leave. . . . Get up there without the loss of a minute. The drive wouldn't take more than two and a half hours, but there were difficulties. Gerald was due back in New York and would probably come here to the house, and Hugh Clavering might call. If she wasn't home an alarm might be raised. . . . It was the last thing in the world she wanted. No one must know about Harvey or where he was until she'd had a chance to talk to him. Madge was the answer.

She said, "Madge, if Gerald Straws calls you, or Hugh Clavering, tell them about the station wagon and that I've gone up to the farm, but don't tell anyone else." Madge said she would

"You're going now?" she asked, and Dace said yes. "It's not quite three, and I can be there well before six. I'll call the superintendent in Gerald's apartment house and Hugh Clavering's hotel and leave a message for them to call you, and I'll keep in touch with you myself." She hung up, made the two calls and, about to leave the phone, picked it up again. Olivia had said something about coming in that evening after dinner and she'd have to let her know. She felt guilty about Olivia. Her ridiculous suspicion the other day concerning her cousin and Harvey had dissolved into thin air practically before it had taken shape, but it had given her a frightened measure of her own disordered state of mind. That was over. Now she was sane again.

She dialed Olivia's office, got her, and said, "Don't come down tonight, Olivia, I won't be here. I'll explain later." The phone would no longer be monitored—if it ever had been—but it was better to be sure, caution had become a habit with her. At the other end of the wire Olivia was startled and mystified. Then she said, "Harvey?"

"Yes," Dace said, and before she could say any more, Olivia said, "I was leaving here anyhow. Wait for me, Dace, I'll grab a cab and be down there in ten minutes."

Olivia was as good as her word, nevertheless Dace begrudged every second. She was on fire with impatience to be moving. She threw some things into a case, and put on a dark wool dress and brogues. She was downstairs again and about to call the garage when Olivia arrived. Dace told her quickly about the station wagon and where it had been found and that she was going up to the farm.

Olivia was dismayed. "Oh, Dace," she pleaded, "Not tonight. It's late and it's foggy out, and it'll soon be dark. Why can't you . . . ?"

But Dace was determined. Harvey might not be at the farm but there was a good chance that he was.

"All right," Olivia said firmly, "if you insist on going, you're not going alone. I'm going with you."

Dace didn't argue, besides she was glad to have company. They walked to the garage, it was quicker than having the car delivered. While Dace waited for the Benz to be brought down Olivia telephoned from the drug store on the corner and broke a date with the Bates man for cocktails. A quarter of an hour later, at about the time detective Bronstein was ringing the bell of the house in the court on Murray Hill in vain, the two girls were on the West Side Highway headed north.

The fog delayed them. In spots after it got dark it was really nasty and in places they had to slow to a crawl. The drive ordinarily took about two and a half hours; that night it took almost four. It was twenty minutes past eight when they turned through the farm gates and started up the winding driveway, the headlights cutting a swath through the mist. It was thick in the bottoms, thinner higher up. When they rounded the final turn Dace scrutinized the long façade of the house crowning the rise, with anxious eyes, and her heart sank. There were no lights on anywhere.

They had shared the driving and Olivia was at the wheel. Leaning over to turn off the ignition her elbow struck the horn. In the profound stillness, the desolation and emptiness confronting them, the blast made both girls jump. It was too loud and too bold, a summons to nothing. Olivia said irritably, "Damn," and they both got out, mechanically stretching and flexing muscles, stiff from sitting still so long. Dace stood looking up at the house front. Not a light in any window, not so much as a gleam, and Harvey hated darkness. . . . Wherever he was he kept the lights blazing. They had had their journey for nothing. She was suddenly very tired. She said blankly, "It's no good—I don't think Harvey's here."

Olivia was not so easily defeated. "How do we know whether he is or not? He may be in a room at the back, or maybe he's outside somewhere. We'll be able to tell better when we look around inside. Come on."

At first it didn't seem as though they were going to be able to get inside the house at all. Madge had given Dace a set of keys before they left the farm on Wednesday morning but when Dace tried the one for the front door, selecting it in the light from the headlamps, the door wouldn't open. It was evidently bolted on the inside. So was the door to the north wing. They finally got in through the barn; the door there was not bolted.

Dace used the key, and the door opened easily on darkness. There was a switch to the left of it. Olivia held a match for her and she found the switch and pushed it. Nothing happened. She said, "The electricity must be off. Mr. Neibold must have turned it off when he closed the house."

"There must be a main switch somewhere, Dace."

"I suppose so, but we'll never find it in the dark."

"Wait a minute," Olivia said. "There's a flashlight in the

glove compartment in the car. I saw it when I was searching for matches. You stay here and I'll go and get it."

Her footsteps receded. The blackness was intense and the chill bitter. There wasn't a sound anywhere beyond the half-open door to the passageway that led past a game room to the kitchen regions. Surely if Harvey was here he would have turned on the oil furnace and the electricity, Dace thought. But perhaps not, perhaps he'd be afraid to. Afraid of what? A chill that had nothing to do with the icy air struck through her. A car door slammed distantly. Olivia was coming back. Dace let air out of her lungs and began to breathe normally.

Light made all the difference. "Here we are." Joining her, Olivia sent a funnel of brilliance ahead of them along the passageway, sent it stabbing over the game room, the ping-pong and billiard tables, the cues in a rack, the chairs—nothing and no one. On along the passageway to the door into the kitchen; the moment they opened the kitchen door it came out to meet them—heat, a great wave of it.

Olivia gave an exclamation and pushed light around. Objects leaped into view and faded back into obscurity, white enamel and Monel metal and green tiling, cabinets, counters, sinks, the long stove fueled by bottled gas. Quick with excitement Dace crossed to the stove and put her hand on the oven.

It was hot to the touch. The gas was off but it had been lit a short time ago. Harvey must have lit it. It couldn't be anyone else. He must be here. She said so. Olivia said, "Yes—or he was. What about that station wagon, Dace? Before we go any farther do you think we ought to drive down to that old barn and see if the station wagon's still there?"

Surely if Harvey was in the house he would have heard them, Dace thought. They had made plenty of noise. "Perhaps we'd better," she said. "Let's go out this way, it's shorter." She crossed to the back kitchen door, pushed back the bolt and opened the door. Olivia sent torch light ahead of them for their feet, and gave a cry, and stood still.

The black and white station wagon was there, just

outside on the gravel. It was empty. There was no one behind the wheel. The keys were in the ignition and the engine was faintly warm. The two girls looked at each other. They didn't need to say anything. Harvey was, he must be, somewhere in the house, or at least in its immediate vicinity.

Dace took the keys out of the ignition and dropped them into her pocket. She said it was possible that Harvey might be asleep in one of the upstairs rooms, which would explain why he hadn't heard them, and Olivia agreed. Unconsciously they both kept their voices low. Returning to the kitchen, they went through it and on into the big, cavernous dining room, and were momentarily stopped. The door into the living room was bolted on the inside. They went back into the kitchen, through it and on into the utility room. Deep-Freeze on the left, huge icebox on the right, more counters and sinks. There were two doors, one to the dining room and the other to the great central living room. Both of these doors were locked. None of the keys Dace had would open them. They were shut out of the body of the house.

Olivia snapped her fingers. "The back stairs," she said. "Maybe we can get in that way. Come on."

The door at the top of the stairs wasn't locked. Torch light prodding and poking into the three bedrooms in the north wing; they were all silent and empty. On down the corridor that gave on the balcony running around the living room, the south wing remained. They didn't have to search the south wing. Before they reached the door to the balcony they heard it, clear and sweet. A man was whistling somewhere fairly close by.

Harvey . . . Dace had the door to the balcony open, was out on the balcony. Light combating light, the torch was no longer necessary. She stepped to the railing, Olivia crowding her shoulder, and they both looked down.

Harvey was there, below them, in profile, stretched out in a long chair to the right of the fire. He had just put a match to it. Flames crept and cracked. He sat looking at the fire, his eyes on it, his head back against the cushions, his feet on a leather footstool, relaxed and at ease. Beside him on the table at his elbow there was a half-empty flask of whiskey and a glass.

Dace understood in a flash what had happened. Harvey had been down in the cellar turning on the electricity when they were in the kitchen regions. That was why he hadn't heard them, he didn't know they were there. . . . about to call to him her throat opened, and closed. Sudden thought stopped the cry at her lips. She had the keys of the station wagon but the Benz keys were in that car parked near the front door.

She put a quick hand on Olivia's arm, put her lips close to Olivia's ear. "The Benz, the keys."

Olivia understood. If only Harvey didn't rouse and look up and see them they could get to the Benz and take the keys in case he decided to run again before they had time to tell him that everything was all right, that he was no longer in any danger, that the warrant for his arrest had been quashed.

Holding their breath they started around the balcony toward the stairs. It was the quickest way. Harvey's back was turned. Dace kept her eyes on the top of his head. He didn't move, didn't hear them, the rugs were thick, he kept on staring into the fire. Then the overhang of the balcony hid him from view. They crept on.

They were within two yards of the stairs and a dash for the front door and the Benz when it happened. Olivia dropped the now useless flashlight. It fell with a resounding thud, rolled to the railing and through it and down into the living room where it crashed into something. Then Harvey did move. The scrape of a heel, and then a click. The lights went out.

It was like being struck suddenly blind. "Harvey," Dace cried in a strangled voice she scarcely recognized as her own, and began to run. The top of the stairs in blackness, the railing under her hand, her pounding feet. Too late for the car now. "Harvey, it's me, Dace," she called again, and slipped and slid and regained her balance.

It was the slip that did it. Olivia caromed into her from behind and they were both falling headlong. One clear moment of consciousness; Dace heard the crack as her forehead struck the hardness of wood. She didn't hear the long sigh in the sudden stillness that followed, she heard nothing at all.

Awareness of a sort came back to Dace fragmentarily

140

at some point farther along. It was getting late, very late indeed, and there wasn't much time left, she knew that. She knew also that there was something she ought to do about it, but she couldn't think what. . . . She wandered on in blackness in a long, dark tunnel. A mine. A coal mine deep in the earth. It was very cold. No, it wasn't, it was roasting hot. Funny thing, that. The tunnel had turned into a lake and she was lying face down in it. It was warm water, salty and thick. She had to buy some air. . . . The storekeeper was out of it. A trap door came down and hit her, pressing her deeper into the sticky water. Go to sleep, she thought, that was the easiest . . . She slept.

Mr. and Mrs. Joseph Gans were just finishing a late dinner in their house a mile down the road from the Allert farm when a strange man raced past the living-room windows, rang the bell furiously and then began hammering on the front door. Mr. Gans threw down his napkin and went to answer the abrupt and startling summons. A tall man charged in without being asked. He wasn't a vagrant, his clothes were good. He was out of breath. "Like to—use your phone. There's been some trouble. . . . I want to call the police."

"Oh—over here." Gans led him to the telephone. "Quickest way is to tell the operator."

"Yes." The stranger dialed. The operator gave him the state barracks. He had his breath back, spoke concisely, first identifying himself. "My name is Clavering. Will you send men to the Allert Farm on Stony Hill Road as fast as you can? There's trouble there. I'll meet you at the farm. I'm talking from a house down the road. The Allert phone is out of order. . . . Hurry, will you, it's urgent."

Less than ten minutes later two state troopers arrived at the farm and found Hugh Clavering pacing up and down on the gravel in front of the long white house high on the hill under leafless trees, bits of fog clinging to their branches. A quick interchange: "You the man who phoned?" "That's right." "What seems to be the trouble?" As the three men advanced on the door at the head of a low flight of wide, shallow steps Clavering explained.

He had had a message from Mrs. Allert that she and her cousin were coming up here from New York tonight

141

and he had followed them. When he got to the house he found it in darkness. Their car, a Benz, wasn't there, but the front door was unlocked. He had gone inside and switched the lights on. There was no sign of Mrs. Allert and her cousin anywhere but the fire was lit and . . .

He went through the door first. "Come and I'll show you. Over here."

The two troopers went with him across the huge room toward the stairs leading up to the balcony. Clavering pulled up short and pointed down.

There was blood on the floor at the bottom of the steps, on the shining oak boards and on the edge of the rug. While they were standing there looking at the wet redness the front door opened again. It was thrown open, and another man came walking into the room. It was Gerald Straws. He explained his arrival hastily. He had come on the same errand as Clavering, and by the same means, a message from Dace waiting for him at his apartment to call Madge Tarbel in Vermont. Madge had told him where the two girls were making for. He stared at the blood silently, his face as grim as those of the others, then they were all in motion.

A quick search of the house, of the other rooms upstairs and down, of the barn, the stables, was unproductive. There was one catch and an important one, the black and white station wagon drawn up outside the back door. But it was empty. There was no sign of Mrs. Allert or her cousin, no sign that they had been at the house at all until Gerald Straws saw the flashlight Olivia had dropped, lying under a table below the balcony in the living room. He said, "They were here all right, that flashlight was in the Benz. I know because I gave it to Harvey, and it was kept in the glove compartment."

A narrower scrutiny of the room disclosed the faint trail of blood stains, almost invisible on the red of the rug. It led toward the door under the stairs, set in the paneling in such a way that it attracted no attention. "The closet!" Both Clavering and Straws said that at the same moment, and dashed for it.

The closet was locked. A couple of minutes and a crowbar from the barn pried it open. The two women were there, on the floor, half under a pile of coats that had

142

fallen on them. They were unconscious, and a terrible sight, but not dead. There was blood all over them; Dace's face was a mask of redness. It came from a wound in her forehead.

The telephone that Hugh Clavering had vainly tried to use when he first got to the house had been pulled out by the roots from the wall behind the desk on which it stood. A message for help, for a doctor and an ambulance and reinforcements, was sent over the radio on the police car while the other trooper and Clavering and Straws lifted the two girls out gently and laid them on the rug with pillows under their heads. The closet was small and airless and lined tightly with cedar; another hour or so and they would have been done for.

Olivia recovered consciousness first. She opened her eyes, gave a long sigh, blinked at the light and at the trooper bending over her, and tried to sit up. "Where's Harvey . . . ? Where . . . ?" It was too much trouble. Her head fell back on the pillow.

Brandy from a flask the trooper put to her lips brought her to again. In a couple of minutes she was able to talk, disjointedly. They had come up here to the farm, they had found Harvey, and then the lights had gone out and they had fallen down the stairs.

Harvey Allert—the troopers looked at each other. The alarm was out for Harvey Allert, an urgent alarm, not this time for forgery, there was a homicide number attached. It had come in over the teletype hours earlier, and at around three o'clock one of the scout cars had patrolled over here but there was no sign of Allert or of the black and white station wagon, and the house itself was closed up tight.

At that point Dace opened her eyes. The first person she saw was Hugh Clavering. He was kneeling beside her, holding her hands and chafing them. There was the tension of pain, of agony, in his face. It began to clear as she looked up at him. "Thank God," he said, "thank God . . . No, don't try to talk, don't say anything, just rest, Dace, rest . . ." Her eyelids fell.

Reinforcements were arriving, a carload of troopers from the barracks, a doctor, and then an ambulance. The two women couldn't be examined properly there; they were removed to the hospital in Poughkeepsie. Gerald

Straws and Hugh Clavering drove off after them as soon as they had answered a few more questions, and the police got down to work.

What Olivia Wood had said, plus various other things, had given them enough to set the picture. Harvey Allert had been at the farm and Harvey Allert was gone, but his movements up to the time of his departure weren't hard to figure out—in the light of what had transpired the night before. After killing Floss Crosby in the Hotel Charles in Danbury Allert fled from the hotel and drove across country in the black and white station wagon. It was only a matter of forty odd miles or so. The station wagon had become a liability; he had been linked with it by the ticket he had received late the previous Tuesday night. So he put the telltale car under cover, safely as he thought, in the old barn in the back field.

His intention had probably been to hide out in the house until the hue and cry over Floss Crosby's death died down and he could figure some way of, one, returning home if no suspicions concerning him had been aroused, or, two, of getting out of the country altogether. He might have succeeded in lying low on the farm for a considerable time if it hadn't been for the arrival of his wife and her cousin. It must have been a terrific shock to him to find them unexpectedly not only in the house but looking down at him from the balcony. He had had no warning of their presence, he had been down in the cellar—the dust on the steps was disturbed—attending to the electricity, which had either gone off accidentally or which had been turned off; the Deep-Freeze and the refrigerator were on a separate line of their own. He had then come up to the big central living room to sit before the fire in comfort with the bottle of bourbon. He had already had some of it: the glass had been used, and there were prints on glass, bottle and chair arms which would undoubtedly turn out to be his.

Surprised by the two women his first movement had been to switch off the lights and plunge the room into darkness. The fall they had had down the stairs in the sudden blackness had made any further attack on them unnecessary; they were out for the count. He had dragged them across the rug and over to the closet, a distance of not more than fifteen feet, dumped them inside and locked the door. He had ripped out the telephone wires just in case, and had then taken off in his own car; the Benz was standing waiting and ready outside the front door.

Allert realized that the alarm for his wife and her cousin would be raised sooner or later but he probably didn't expect it to come so fast—in all likelihood figuring that he had the whole night ahead of him in which to ditch the Benz and find some other means of conveyance or some other hiding hole. He wasn't going to get far.

Hugh Clavering had alerted the barracks at shortly after nine P.M., and the alarm for the convertible was out before ten. Give him at best a two-hour start; the two hours weren't going to get him any place. Roadblocks were being set up at strategic spots in a four-state spread, and a thousand eyes would be searching for him throughout the night.

All this was done. The thousand eyes failed. The night passed and there was nothing. Morning came and with morning Inspector McKee and Captain Pierson arrived from New York.

It was the light that did it. In daylight, a gray wintry day with a threat of more snow, as soon as they could see clearly the police picked up the Benz's tracks leading away from the house. The car was heavy, the ground a little softened by fog, and the tires well treaded.

There were three estate roads, or rather lanes, out of the farm sitting high on the hill: one short one to the east; one to the southwest close to the ten-acre field and the old barn in which Allert had hidden the station wagon; and a third, a mere track along the heights to the north running above and roughly parallel with the river.

It was this road Harvey Allert had taken, but not for long and not far. Broken branches and crushed saplings marked the Benz's abrupt change of course. Less than a quarter of a mile from the house the Benz had swerved from the lane and had gone over the edge of the cliff and down into the narrow, swiftly flowing river.

They located the car. It was lying close to the bank in twelve or fifteen feet of water. They got it up and on shore at four o'clock that afternoon. Harvey Allert's body was not in the Benz. The door on the driver's side was open, and the current between the close-pressing hills was fairly swift there and free of weeds. Allert's body would have been carried downstream. In the middle of the preparation being made to drag the river, the two New York Homicide men left the farm.

Walking toward the car in which they had driven up from New York, in the teeth of an icy wind, Pierson said, "What do you think, Inspector? Was Allert in the Benz—or is it a plant? Did he send the car over the cliff and jump clear and is he off to the races?"

"I don't know," McKee said slowly, eyeing the crowding pine woods dark against the snow. "The spot where he left the lane back there is rocky. No marks on the rocks to give a lead . . . Allert appears to have been an expert driver and he knew the road. I rather doubt whether what happened back there could have been an accident. On the other hand, if Allert intended to kill himself, why did he bother taking time to lock those two women in the closet under the stairs inside the house? They were helpless anyhow, and his way to the car and escape were clear. It doesn't add up. . . . No. But if Harvey Allert did jam the accelerator and jump clear, where does he expect to get, with the whole countryside on the lookout for him? If he's in the river they'll dredge him up, if he isn't—well we'll just have to wait and see. But until then, until we get hold of him, alive or dead . . ."

He paused for a moment in the somber snow light and the keen wind coming off the hills and thought about Mercedes Allert with her small proud head and clear eyes—and went on in a harder voice, "I'll tell you one thing that's got to be done in the meantime—until Harvey Allert is found his wife's got to be watched every minute of the time."

THIRTEEN

Watching Dace Allert adequately proved to be, as McKee had expected, a difficult assignment. She and Olivia had been taken to the hospital Friday night and late on Sunday they were discharged. The wound in Dace's temple, although it had bled a lot, proved to be superficial and there was no concussion; what she and Olivia were both suffering from was shock. Instead of returning to New York the two girls went up to the farm to wait for news.

Madge had come back and the house had been opened and warmed, and the nightmare quality, outwardly at least, banished. But not for Dace. McKee had talked to her at the hospital in Poughkeepsie before going to New York, and she knew it all now, the whole horror of what had happened in the Hotel Charles in Danbury last Thursday night, before Harvey fled to the farm for refuge. Everyone else knew it, too. She was left in no doubt about that.

The wife of a murderer—how does it feel, Mrs. Allert, what are you thinking about? Such a respectable murderer, too, of such good standing in the world, and young and handsome, with just about everything . . . Why did he do it? The money, of course. He must have killed his stepmother, he certainly killed that poor girl in the

147

hotel in Danbury. How does it make you feel . . . ? Tell us, tell us.

Dace could see this in the eyes of everyone she encountered, the nurses at the hospital, the doctors, the patients in the corridors, and the crowd outside when she and Olivia left the building. Reluctant conviction on the facts was unanimous; it was there in Gerald Straws and in Olivia and in Hugh and in the Longstreets, who had come up from New York and were waiting at the farm.

Joan Longstreet had solved it satisfactorily for herself. She was deeply saddened, but composed and firm. These tragedies occurred and there was nothing that could be done about them. Harvey was not responsible for what he had done for the simple reason that he didn't know what he was doing. Therefore you couldn't blame him. He was mentally deranged, out of his mind. It wasn't the real Harvey who had done those terrible things. It could happen to anyone. "Poor boy, poor boy." Kermit Longstreet said the same thing in a lower, distressed tone.

Among them they had almost convinced Dace, but not quite. She could understand Harvey's shutting Olivia and her into the closet under the stairs, she could even believe that he had killed the girl in the Hotel Charles on impulse, in an uncontrollable fit of fury; what she couldn't bring herself to believe was that he had planned Elfrida's death, deliberately, cold-bloodedly, with minute care, in advance. And yet there was the blanket of daisies which had so shocked her. . . . He had, he hadn't, he wouldn't, he did . . . .

If Harvey's body was in the river, the fast-flowing, ice-choked stream between the hills was reluctant to give up its burden. Two whole days passed in which the dragging produced nothing but a vast mass of rubbish, including the skeleton of a cow. But Harvey Allert had to be in the river. Where else could he be? The nets on land were closer meshed than the ones in the water, and they had been flung wide. If Harvey wasn't in the Benz when it went over the top of the cliff, where could he be concealing himself?

It remained a question mark to Dace as well as the police. He had had less than a three-hour start before the hunt was on. Trains and buses had been eliminated. So

148

had trucks on their regular runs. Private cars remained, but the case had broken wide open and the papers were full of the story. Anyone who had given the wanted man a lift would surely have come forward.

There was a chance that he was hiding in the wooded hills that were thick in that part of the country, keeping ahead of the sporadic searchers, who could easily be seen and heard, dodging them and doubling on his tracks. It was a slim chance. The weather had turned cold again, he had no food, and the overcoat he wore, warm as it was, would be little or no protection against a temperature of a few degrees above zero.

On other fronts the case against Harvey Allert was equally unproductive, wouldn't march. All attempts so far to link Floss Crosby with Harvey Allert had failed. And yet the girl had recognized him when she encountered him in the Charles lobby. More than that, she had greeted him warmly, as a friend. The testimony of Mrs. Christianberry, the woman who had watched the meeting, had been both disinterested and exact. The search for the link between them went on, as did the dragging of the river in Duchess County. And in the big house on the hill under the bare trees the collection of people gathered there waited for news in grim seclusion, cut off from the rest of the world.

McKee had two pairs of watching eyes up there. One pair belonged to detective Todhunter of his own staff, the other to Lucy Sturm, the woman he had managed to introduce into the household without anyone's being aware of what her other function was, besides being a registered nurse. The doctors had advised a nurse for the present, to see how Mrs. Harvey Allert got on. Staying in the house itself were Madge Tarbel, Dace and Olivia, and Joan Longstreet. Kermit Longstreet came and went from the city. Hugh Clavering and Gerald Straws were staying at a motel in the valley but they spent most of their time at the farm, in or about the house. Scott Evans had also put in an appearance. He had a room in the village.

Lucy Sturm had her work cut out for her. Dace absolutely refused to remain in bed. Nor would she stay put anywhere for long. Nor would she listen to anyone. Restlessness drove her, she was a white, unquiet ghost with an expressionless face. She could sit still in any given spot for only a few minutes at a time, then she would be on her feet. And she resented being watched over and followed around by all of them, without exception.

"I'm going for a little walk on the terrace. No, Olivia, don't come with me." "No, Hugh." "No, Gerald." "Miss Sturm, I'd like to be alone, if you don't mind," and on several occasions she practically bared her teeth at Mrs. Longstreet when the latter tried to accompany her. Or she'd go upstairs and her door would close and she'd walk up and down, up and down, you could hear her footsteps, but in a short time she'd be out again and wandering around from room to room.

At the end of the second day Lucy Sturm reported to the Inspector from a booth in the drug store in the village while Todhunter kept guard at the farm. The nurse said, "She's in a bad way, Inspector. I wouldn't be surprised if she cracked, if she tried to do something desperate. . . . Sedatives? Don't worry about that. I'm doling them out one by one, and I see that she takes what I give her so she can't do any stockpiling. . . . Yes, I stick to her as close as I can, but I can't be with her every minute. She's very sweet, I've never met a sweeter girl, and she's so lovely to look at, but she's got a way with her, a strong will, and then she's all to pieces. I'll be glad when this case is over."

Dace knew that she was being rude and savage and ungrateful; she couldn't help it. Harvey a murderer, because conviction was beginning to come at last. She hadn't realized how fond she had been of him with all his faults. To her he had been a child, a wayward, impetuous child with something infinitely pathetic about him. Now they said he was a murderer. . . .

She recoiled from that, tried to run away, run and run—but there was nowhere to run. If only they would find him, if only the search would come to an end, then she could go far away somewhere where no one would know who she was. Murder, the ability to kill—memories of their life together tore at her. How could she not have seen, how could she have been so blind, so stupid? Wrong about that, she could be wrong about everything—and everyone.

Day and daily she took herself to task. She had prided herself on Hugh's love, oh yes she had. She remembered

150

how she had felt in the Rockingham bar just before he told her about Harvey and the check, and again out there in the snow and the cold at the edge of the pine woods, and again the other night when she opened her eyes and saw the agony in his face at the thought that she was dying. It was all gone now. She hadn't known the truth about Harvey—what then did she really know about Hugh, or about Gerald Straws, or any of them? Sometimes she caught herself examining their faces, Joan Longstreet's, and Kermit's, and even Madge's and Scott Evans', and asking herself whether they could kill.

Lucy Sturm wasn't the only one worried about her, the others saw the look in her eyes and discussed it among themselves. Mrs. Longstreet said to her husband, "She's going out of her mind, poor darling, I tell you she *is*." Olivia Wood said with cross weariness, "That's nonsense. It's this waiting that's killing her. I don't see how she can stand much more of it." Hugh Clavering turned on his heel and walked off, his face stone. Gerald Straws agreed somberly that it was the waiting, the suspense that was getting Dace. But she wasn't the only one, they were all keyed up and on edge. You could cut the tension in the house with a knife. It was on Thursday that it finally came to an end.

To Lucy Sturm's relief Dace was quieter that day. She woke late, and the long sleep seemed to have refreshed her. At Madge Tarbel's urging she even ate a little lunch and after lunch she went out for a walk with Hugh Clavering. When he asked her she unexpectedly agreed.

"All right, Hugh, it would be nice to get some air." White face under the soft, dark hair, luminous shadowed eyes, slim figure wrapped in a coat; she and Clavering were walking toward the door, his hand on her arm. It took Lucy Sturm, knitting sedately in the background, by surprise. Lucy put her knitting down and stood.

"Mr. Clavering . . ."

Hugh Clavering smiled at her over his shoulder. He was a very good-looking man, tall and decisive and sure of himself. He saw her anxiety. He said pleasantly, "We won't go far, Nurse, I won't let her tire herself." The door closed behind them.

Lucy was in a quandary. Her bag, with her stock of

drugs and her hypodermic in it, was upstairs in her room, and while the door was locked she hadn't much faith in that—it was an ordinary lock that almost any key would open. If she took time to go upstairs and get the bag she might lose the girl, and McKee's instructions had been firm—Mrs. Allert wasn't to be left alone until Harvey Allert, or Harvey Allert's body, was found. She wasn't alone, Mr. Clavering was with her, but she might shake him off. . . . Lucy went to the closet and got her coat.

Madge Tarbel and Mrs. Longstreet were playing double solitaire at a table under one of the windows and Olivia Wood was reading in a corner of the couch. Yawning and stretching, she looked up as Lucy went past her.

"Going out, Miss Sturm? I think I'll go with you, I could do with a little air myself." She got her coat and tied a scarf over her head and they went out together.

Snow had fallen in the night, a fresh inch or two of it. The pines were green against the snow, and the oaks, which still held some of their leaves, were a deep golden bronze under the cold gray sky. Mrs. Allert and Clavering were in plain view, mounting the hill to the north beyond the outbuildings. Lucy struck off in their wake.

Beside her Olivia said, moving easily through the snow with her long-legged stride, "You're worried about my cousin, aren't you, Miss Sturm?" and Lucy said yes.

"She's not in very good shape. Her nerves are all to pieces, and she hasn't been eating. This is the first day she's touched solid food."

Olivia sighed. "I know. I held my breath at lunch for fear she'd stop. . . . I wish they'd find Harvey. *God*, how I wish they would."

Her voice was strained and her handsome face—she was a very pretty girl—was drawn and unhappy. She had been through a lot, too, Lucy reflected, but she was so much more robust than her cousin that it didn't show.

The two dark figures ahead were almost at the top of the hill. The path they were following skirted the green wall of the pines to the left; to the right the ground fell away into a wide hollow filled with leafless trees and bushes. Mrs. Allert and Clavering would be over the top of the hill in a minute and once over the top they would be out of sight. . . . Lucy Sturm quickened her pace.

152

What happened less than a full minute later was the measure of the tenseness in all of them, herself not excepted.

Hugh Clavering and Mrs. Allert didn't vanish from sight. They had come to a halt and were standing on the crest of the hill, their figures silhouetted against the sky. They stood there in the snow, their backs turned, looking down into the valley through which the river ran, the river that was being dragged for an inert body hidden somewhere in its icy depths. All at once Dace Allert threw out her hands and swayed, and Hugh Clavering put a quick, steadying arm around her shoulders. At the same moment a man began to emerge from the green wall of the pines, perhaps ten feet behind them. First the branches stirred and then a man's head and part of his figure appeared.

Terror seized Lucy Sturm. She thought, Harvey Allert . . . He's been hiding in the woods. . . . They don't know he's there. . . . Stiff with fear, rigid with it, she opened her mouth to shout a warning. Then her muscles came out of spasm and she relaxed weakly.

The man who walked out of the woods wasn't Harvey Allert. It was Mr. Straws. He joined Mrs. Allert and Clavering and all three of them turned and came down the hill together, a man on either side of Mrs. Allert, an arm through hers. At the sight of the river Dace had broken down. There were tears on her face.

Olivia said fiercely to Hugh Clavering, "Hugh, you're a fool—you oughtn't to have taken her there." Dace said, "It's not Hugh's fault, Olivia. I wanted to go, to see . . ." Her eyes had a lost look. Neither Gerald Straws nor Clavering said anything, they had no time for talk, they were both occupied with the girl between them. Three minutes later they were back in the house.

As soon as they got in, the two men took Dace up to her bedroom and there Lucy Sturm assumed command. Mrs. Longstreet bustling up, her husband trailing her, Madge Tarbel, Olivia, and finally Scott Evans, who had just arrived. They were all concerned, worried. Scott Evans kept repeating, "Poor kid, poor kid," with a suggestion of moisture in his eyes.

It was obvious that Dace had had a shock at the sight

of the river. It had brought things home to her. Lucy Sturm closed the door firmly on their anxious faces and Mrs. Longstreet's questions. Taking off her coat and throwing it over a chair, Dace was very white and very quiet. She wouldn't go to bed. She settled herself on a chaise near the windows. "Don't worry about me, Nurse, I'm all right—just tired. I think I'll rest for a while. You don't need to stay."

She didn't want a drink, she didn't want anything. Lucy Sturm was a firm believer in tea. She said, "You lie there and rest and relax and take it easy, Mrs. Allert. I'm going to make you a nice cup of tea, it will make you feel much better."

The back stairs were just beyond Dace's room. Lucy went down to the kitchen. It only took a minute for the water to boil. She didn't bother with a teapot, she used a tea bag.

When she got upstairs Dace was just as she had left her, lying on the chaise, her head against the cushions, her shadowed eyes on the wintry hills and fields being swallowed up gradually by the beginnings of dusk. When Dace had taken a pill obediently she drank the tea thirstily. "That was good. Thank you." She handed the empty cup back and said she thought she'd try and get a little sleep.

Lucy said it was an excellent idea. "I'll see that no one disturbs you." She went out and closed the door softly behind her.

Voices drifted up faintly from the living room. The long corridor was dim. Lucy switched on a lamp midway along its length, took the cup down to the kitchen and rinsed it out, returned upstairs, went into her own room next to Dace's and then—and only then—checked on her bag.

Her bag wasn't in the closet, or anywhere else in the room. Her bag was gone.

Besides the usual drugs and a thermometer and a hypodermic and a supply of fresh needles, the small bag had various sedatives and some ampules of morphine in it. . . . Lucy Sturm wasn't a woman who panicked easily—she had been in difficult situations before—but panic touched her then. She shook it off and tried to think. But a conclusion was hard to arrive at. Anyone could have got into her room with one of the other bedroom keys. To slip in here, pick up the bag and slip out again would have taken only a few seconds. She went on thinking.

The Longstreets and Madge Tarbel had remained in the house while she had been following Mrs. Allert and Clavering. . . . And since she had come back in, there were those two journeys to the kitchen while they were all there. . . .

Thinking was a waste of time. She wiped a damp palm on her uniform. The missing bag and its contents was a fact—what was she to do about it?

She still held the key with which she had unlocked her own door, the now useless key, in her fingers. It was better than nothing. Lock Mrs. Allert's door, she decided, collect what other keys she could find, and then go out and get hold of Todhunter and tell him what had happened.

Out in the corridor she listened at Dace's door. There wasn't a sound from inside the room. The poor girl had probably dozed off. . . . Lucy Sturm started to fit the key into the lock. It was loose, rattled around. At the first tinkle of metal Mrs. Allert stirred. The springs of the chaise creaked, and she murmured something drowsily. Then there was no further sound. She had evidently nodded off again.

The nurse drew back the key as though it were made of dynamite and dropped it into her pocket. If Mrs. Allert came fully awake and found herself locked in, there was no telling what she might do. And nothing could happen while she herself was away—it wouldn't take more than a minute or two to get hold of Todhunter; the little detective stayed close to the house, within call. The long corridor was dim. Shadows banked it beyond the small pool of lamplight—nothing moved, and there was no one in sight. Lucy Sturm went down the back stairs fast on tiptoe and let herself out.

Inside her room lying on the chaise with her eyelids drooping—the pill was beginning to take effect—Dace heard Lucy Sturm retreat. The house was very still. There was only a handful of light left in the western sky low on the horizon. The winter nights came down quickly. Sleep and forget, she thought, sleep . . . She closed her eyes. She was very tired, and she began to drift off. . . . All at once

155

she sat up sharply. Someone was tapping on her door.

Dace's heart thudded. "Who's there?" she called, and sat up.

There was no answer except the repeated soft tapping. She tossed the blanket aside, got off the chaise and started across the floor.

Outside in what was all but night Lucy Sturm couldn't find the little detective who had spent long, cold days in the immediate vicinity of the house, drifting about as inconspicuously as a dry leaf. Sometimes he took refuge from the cold in the barn, sometimes in the stables opening out of it, but he was always within reach. He wasn't in either the barn or the stable, he wasn't anywhere in sight on the snowy lawn in front or back. Passing the kitchen windows Lucy saw Miss Tarbel, and the tall, bony woman who had come up from the village to help, making preparations for dinner and went plodding on.

Where could Todhunter *be?* He wouldn't leave the grounds without a very strong reason. She simply had to find him, the Inspector had to be told that her bag had been removed from her room between two and four o'clock that afternoon. There was enough stuff in it to put three or four people to sleep—permanently.

The air was biting. She began to go at a jog trot. She circled the house completely, twice, in case she and the little detective were playing ring around the rosy with each other. There was no sign of Todhunter anywhere, it was useless; she finally gave up and reëntered the house through the front door. Now she'd have to take things into her own hands.

Flattened cushions and used ash trays, a paper thrown down; there was no one there. The big living room was empty in lamp and firelight. Closing the front door behind her Lucy glanced uneasily up the stairs in the direction of Dace's room. No, she thought, the telephone first. The Inspector had to be told about her bag. If anyone overheard her phoning it would break her cover, but that couldn't be helped. She crossed to the phone, picked up the handset and dialed operator. She got the office after a few minutes delay. And Inspector McKee wasn't there. When she identified herself the man at the other end of the wire said the Inspector was in Silverbridge.

Lucy dropped the instrument in its cradle and thought some more. The Inspector mightn't want the information about her bag broadcast. She knew the way he worked, sometimes a thing like this could break a case. Her orders were clear. She was to keep Mercedes Allert safe. As long as she stood between Mrs. Allert and the person who had taken the bag nothing serious could happen Absolutely not.

Some of the tenseness went out of Lucy. If McKee was up here in the country he was probably at the state police barracks, or in touch with the barracks. She picked the phone up and called the state police. But the Inspector wasn't there. She gave her name, left a message asking him to ring her as soon as possible, hung up, and moved away from the telephone. There was no one in sight that she could see, but someone could have been watching and listening from the shadowy balcony above.

There was no evidence of it. She mounted the stairs, turned left toward the south wing and jerked to a sharp halt in the mouth of it, staring in front of her.

The long corridor was in darkness—and she had left the lamp lit on a table halfway along its length. The lamp was off. Lucy Sturm ran. She threw open Mrs. Allert's door and switched on the lights. The room was empty.

By that time Dace was well away from the house. When she had opened her door a good seven or eight minutes earlier at the summons of that soft, insistent tapping, it was to find Hugh standing outside in the dark corridor. She could just barely see him.

"Dace, get a coat. Hurry."

That was all he said. His voice was low, clipped. There was urgency in it. He didn't want to be overheard. . . . Something had happened. Harvey, she thought. It was Harvey. . . . Had they found him, or . . . ? "Is it . . . ?" She shaped his name with difficulty.

"Yes," Hugh said, looking up and down the dark corridor and listening, his head tilted. He had his overcoat on, the collar turned up. "We mustn't be seen. Hurry."

Dace flew to the closet, pulled out her coat and threw it on. Hugh led the way to the top of the back staircase and down it. There were people in the kitchen. Pots and pans rattled and someone said something about mashed potatoes. Hugh opened the heavy outside door, looked around, beckoned Dace out and closed the door behind her, softly.

A pale expanse of snow ran toward the darkness of the woods; there was still a little light. Hugh took her arm. He didn't strike across the snowy lawn. He turned left, hugging the obscurity under the house walls, then right into the dense shadow of a row of tall pines that formed a windbreak to the north. He was moving fast, just not running, and he kept looking around him, his head turning from side to side. Where was Harvey? Was he alive? If he was, had Hugh found his hiding place? The snow-covered ground underfoot was rough, hummocky. Dace hadn't taken time to put on boots and her feet were cold. The air was bitter and a wind was beginning to rise. It blew loose snow in little puffs and eddies.

All at once Hugh stood still, pulling Dace into a deeper patch of shadow under the trees. There was someone coming toward them. Footsteps breaking through the icy crust below the top layer of whiteness, running footsteps, and then a vague, hurrying figure. It was the nurse. Lucy Sturm passed within fifteen feet of where they stood motionless, then she disappeared around the corner of the house.

Dace was shivering. She couldn't control it. "Hugh . . ." she said, and didn't get any further. He said, "Not now, later. We've got to get clear. . . . My car's not far away. . . . You're cold. Here, take a drink of this." He unscrewed the top of a flask he took from his pocket, handed the flask to her. "Take a drink, don't take a sip. Get it down."

Dace obeyed. The liquor burned in her throat and then in her stomach. The warmth felt good. "More," Hugh urged and she tilted the flask again. The metal was ice under her stiff fingers; Hugh had gloves on, her hands were bare. He took the flask from her, dropped it back into his pocket and they were off again. Hugh led the way now, there wasn't room for two on the narrow, twisting path.

Plunging along blindly at his heels Dace kept on thinking about Harvey. How had Hugh found him—he

158

must be alive because Hugh wouldn't be taking her to him if he wasn't. Was he hurt, dying perhaps? Was that why Hugh had come to get her like this? The path had broadened out and Hugh had hold of her arm again. A deeper darkness now, they had entered the woods without her noticing. . . . Less than half a minute brought them to Hugh's car. He put her into the car and closed the door on her side without making a sound. Then he was beside her behind the wheel and they were moving off.

Hugh didn't turn the headlights on. He sat forward over the wheel, glancing alternately at the snowy track just barely visible under the wheels and into the rearview mirror. His intentness, the narrow concentration in him were frightening. "Hugh," Dace demanded, "where are we going? Where . . . ?"

"In a minute, Dace." He didn't relax, he kept his attention exclusively on the lane in front and behind. The woods began to thin, fields came faintly into sight, then they were at the south gate and through it and out on the smoothness of the side road. Hugh switched on the headlights and put his foot down on the accelerator.

Trees and bushes flying by, they were going very fast. Dace felt light-headed. It was the liquor, she had swallowed a big drink. . . . "Hugh," she demanded again with a tongue not quite under control, "where are you taking me?"

He didn't answer, didn't turn his head.

Looking at his profile, the dark gleam of his eyes fixed ahead of him, the tenseness of his jaw, fear struck into Dace for the first time, fear of Hugh. . . . But Hugh wouldn't—hurt her. . . . Why should he? Bewilderment and anger mingled with the rising tide of fear. Hugh had said he was taking her to Harvey. . . . No, he hadn't. She had said, "Harvey?" and he had just said yes. . . . Her mouth and lips were oddly dry. It was difficult to speak, but she managed it.

"Hugh, if you don't stop this car and tell me where we're going, I'm going to jump out."

"Do you want to be a dead woman, Dace?"

He said it quite calmly, almost sadly. A dead woman—dead . . . Her vision was blurry. The headlights were on but they were dimmer. . . . She could scarcely see.

. . . Something was happening to her. . . . Everything had moved away. She was dwindling in size. She was tiny—she went out.

"All right, Mr. Clavering, you can pull up now. Not too fast—easy does it, we don't want a skid, you know."

Kneeling in the back of the car Todhunter pressed his gun gently between Hugh Clavering's shoulder blades. A single sharp exclamation from Clavering, and that was all. He obeyed. There wasn't anything else he could do, a gun was a great persuader. The car slowed, stopped. Todhunter kept the gun where it was. "Now turn around and drive back the way you came."

Young Mrs. Allert appeared to be asleep. Todhunter was worried about her. She was slumped down on the cushions in an uncomfortable position, her head lolling. It couldn't be helped—there was nothing he could do for her there, and it wouldn't take long to reach the house.

The reason Lucy Sturm hadn't been able to find Todhunter earlier was because he had been otherwise occupied with Hugh Clavering. He had seen Hugh Clavering leaving the farm, apparently for the night, less than half an hour earlier. Clavering didn't leave the farm. As soon as he was out of sight of the house, instead of going on around the curve and down the hill to the main gates and the road to his motel in the village, he had turned right. Following on foot in the dusk Todhunter had come on Clavering's empty car parked without lights in the little-used lane that ran through the pine woods to the south gate. The keys were in the ignition. About to remove the keys Todhunter stayed his hand when he heard Clavering and Mrs. Allert coming along the lane in the darkness under the close-pressing trees.

He decided that it would be nice to know what was going on. He was a small man and it had been no trick at all to conceal himself on the floor in the back of the car. It was Mrs. Allert's collapse that had flushed him out into the open.

The little detective looked at her huddled figure, dark head swaying drunkenly. "What did you give her, Mr. Clavering?"

Clavering said with cold savagery, "Damn you for stopping us. Damn you. You'll regret it. I wanted to get

160

her out of that house, that's all."

"What did you give her?"

"Nothing but a sedative."

"O.K. Move along a little faster."

Three minutes later they reached the house and pulled up before the front door. Todhunter said, "Put your hand on the horn and keep it there, Mr. Clavering."

At the sound of the first long blast the front door opened and Lucy Sturm came running out and down the steps. She was followed by Madge Tarbel and Olivia Wood. Mrs. Allert was lifted from the car and taken inside and carried upstairs to her room. She woke when they touched her but she was groggy with sleep. Her eyes kept closing.

The doctor was sent for. He arrived and examined her. He said she was in no danger. Pulse and respiration were a bit slow but that was only natural. She had had a pill with her tea, besides the sedative Clavering had given her in the brandy, and the best thing to do was let her sleep it off.

Lucy Sturm's missing bag was in the back seat of Hugh Clavering's car.

Todhunter questioned Clavering in one of the drawing rooms on the first floor. Except for a couple of the pills dissolved in brandy that Clavering had given Dace, the contents of the bag, contents which could be lethal, were intact. Clavering curtly denied taking the bag from Lucy Sturm's room. He said he had found it when he left the house that afternoon, lying in a clump of bushes near where his car was parked.

A likely story. Todhunter said, "Why did you drug Mrs. Allert?"

"So she wouldn't get out of the car, do anything foolish."

"Why did you take her away from here?"

"Because she isn't safe. I don't believe Allert's dead—and he's a killer. He may try to get hold of Dace—perhaps use her as a shield in a getaway. The man's desperate, he's more than that—he's mad, and he won't stop at anything. . . ."

Brilliant improvisation, or the truth as the fellow saw it? It wasn't Todhunter's business to evaluate, that was for the Inspector.

"You can stop worrying about Harvey Allert, Mr. Clavering."

"What do you mean . . . ? You've got him?"

"Yes."

Clavering's outburst of relief was genuine. "Thank God for that. . . . Now we can all breathe again." The tension went out of him, the tension of a man who has been running a long race and who has somehow managed to stumble over the finish line.

He threw himself back in his chair, lit a cigarette, and inhaled smoke deeply. "Dead?"

Todhunter nodded and told him.

Harvey Allert's body had been recovered from the river into which he had plunged five nights ago, at half past ten that morning, in what was to have been one of the last three drags. The autopsy was in progress.

By that time the others, with the exception of Dace, had all been informed, Joan Longstreet, who had gone to meet her husband and came in with him, burst into tears with no regard for her make-up, and refused to be consoled at first, but later her common sense got the upper hand of her grief, so that she was able to have a drink and eat a little dinner. She said through her tears that it was better this way, far, far better for Harvey, poor boy—poor, poor boy.

As for the rest of them, although they had been waiting for this news for days, it was still a shock. Olivia Wood's eyes were red-rimmed with crying and Gerald Straws was hard hit, and showed it—he and Harvey Allert had been boys together. Scott Evans, who had come to the house for dinner, broke down openly and applied himself morosely to the Scotch for support and comfort. Madge Tarbel also wept; she had known Harvey since he was six years old.

McKee didn't arrive at the farm until nine o'clock that evening, and then he only stayed a short time. The autopsy was still going on but certain things had already been established. Joan Longstreet was wrong. Harvey Allert hadn't taken his own life. He had defeated justice in another way, not of his own choosing. He hadn't died by drowning, he hadn't suffocated, there was no bloody froth in his lungs. Nor had he committed suicide. Fleeing the

162

house five nights earlier, after he locked Dace and Olivia in the closet under the stairs, Harvey had died at the wheel of his car of a massive coronary thrombosis. When the car went out of control and over the edge of the cliff and down into the river, he was already dead.

As far as the police were concerned there were still a number of loose ends to be tied up. Although everybody would be there anyhow, before leaving the house that night, just to make sure, McKee said he would want to talk to them all in the morning. He went upstairs and had a look at Dace, who was deeply asleep, and he had a word with Lucy Sturm. The nurse knew where her bag had been found.

She said, "Did Mr. Clavering take it to make me leave Mrs. Allert alone and go searching for it so he could get at her, Inspector?"

The Scotsman shrugged. "I don't know. It doesn't matter now. . . . Just stay with her, don't leave her at all." When he went out of the room he closed the door behind him. Downstairs again some five minutes later, getting into his coat and picking up his hat, the only thing he said to Todhunter was, "Stay awake and keep your eyes open," and let himself out.

FOURTEEN

Harvey Allert's body had been raised to the surface, pulled ashore and taken to the town mortuary in the middle of the morning. As soon as McKee got the flash in New York he had had a talk with Lieutenant Murray, who was in command of the local state barracks in that part of Duchess County. Murray agreed to have the autopsy performed at once. "With particular attention to the contents of the stomach you say, Inspector?"

"That's right, Lieutenant. I'll be along presently." The Scotsman was anxious to get up to Silverbridge, but he didn't leave the city for another three hours.

The night before, seated at his desk in the long, narrow inner office, his feet on the radiator, his hands clasped behind his head, he had gone back over every bit of evidence in the Allert case, a case which wasn't his but in which his interest had steadily grown. With Dwyer's handwriting men in disagreement about the check for a thousand dollars forged on Elfrida Allert's account, the Scotsman had gone to Livingston himself. For McKee's money, although he was in his seventies, Livingston was the best there was.

And Livingston had given it as his opinion, cautiously, that while the check was a forgery he had some doubt

164

about Harvey Allert's being the forger, admitting at the same time that he could be wrong.

If Harvey Allert hadn't forged the check, this set up a whole new range of values. . . . McKee abandoned the check and returned to the man himself. They had never been able to quite catch up with Harvey Allert, he had always been one step ahead of the police, a fatal step as far as the killing in the Hotel Charles in Danbury went. Collusion—as had crossed his mind earlier? It looked more probable than ever that Allert had been kept informed of what was being done in his absence, and what was going on, by someone on the inside so that he could angle his moves.

To the north, beyond the office window, the wintry darkness was distantly spangled with the brilliance of flashing neon signs that put out the stars. BIMS FOR INDIGESTION . . . DRINK KISCO . . . SAY SERVICE AND YOU SAY SUTTERS . . . THE FOUNTAIN OF YOUTH, RAVEN RIVER ORANGE JUICE, STRAIGHT FROM THE GROVES TO YOU . . . Beneath this display a golden fountain spouted golden balls in an endless falling cascade.

The fountain of youth . . . McKee's eyes focused on the golden balls. A spark began at the back of them. Again he sent his mind step by step over Harvey Allert's procedure from the day he bolted out of the Murray Hill house in New York until, in the same car, his own car, he went over the cliff to his death in the river more than a week later. The idea floating around in McKee's mind began slowly to take shape. The spark at the back of his eyes grew. It was possible. . . . It could be. . . . He took his feet off the radiator, swiveled around, and pressed his buzzer.

A good deal of work had been done since that time. The first thing that had been retrieved was the dark blue vicuña overcoat Harvey Allert had worn when he left the house in the court on Murray Hill on the afternoon of his stepmother's fatal crash. Returning to the house the following night to get money, Allert had changed his clothes, leaving the dark blue affair behind and wearing the tan tweed ulster, which was thicker and warmer, away from the house. McKee hadn't bothered with a court order, he had called Beecham the first thing that morning, well before Harvey Allert's body had been finally found. Beecham said, "Certainly you can take the coat, as far as I'm concerned. Go right ahead—but I don't see what good it'll do you."

More men had been sent to talk to the people in Harvey Allert's office. Allert had come in late on that Thursday almost two weeks ago, and he had left early to take a client to lunch. The client was a Mr. Brubaker, the account man for Liberstraum Woolens. Mr. Brubaker was the man the Scotsman wanted to get hold of.

Unfortunately Mr. Brubaker was not immediately available, he was vacationing in Florida, address unknown. He had to be found. Everything now depended on Brubaker and what Brubaker had to say. Finding him might take a little time.

He hadn't been located when McKee left New York for Silverbridge on the afternoon of the day Harvey Allert's body was recovered. It wasn't until ten o'clock on the following morning that Brubaker was finally contacted. At a few minutes after eleven A.M. McKee swung through the gates of the Allert farm and up the hill to the long white house surrounded by leafless trees. He was accompanied by Captain Pierson of his own squad, Lieutenant Murray and two state troopers.

When McKee went through the front door he knew the how and why of the murder of Floss Crosby in the Danbury hotel, and what had really happened to Elfrida Allert. He didn't know the most important thing of all—but it would be along shortly. Messages from the lab in New York would come straight here to the farm. Meanwhile he wanted all these people under his hand, and he wanted rather more precise information than he had been originally given, if he could get it.

It was a hostile and guarded group of people he confronted in the huge living room that morning. They couldn't, or wouldn't, understand this display of police, in force, when it was all over, when the case was closed. Harvey was dead and he couldn't be brought to account for anything he had done. Why pile more opprobrium on him, and why harrow their feelings further? They had all been through the mill and were now entitled to a decent privacy. The intrusion was nothing less than an outrage.

The only exception to the coldness and deep distaste with which McKee was regarded, by the Longstreets, Scott Evans, Clavering and Gerald Straws, and even Madge Tarbel, was Mercedes Allert herself.

As far as Dace was concerned, the reason she sat so still, her eyes empty in her small white face, was that she was bemused, drained, there was no emotion left in her for outside affairs, and everything was outside. Harvey had been found. Harvey was dead. She would never know now what had driven him on in his madness, or how far she was responsible. The torturing uncertainty would be with her forever. She viewed the room and the people in it apathetically. Gerald Straws biting on a cold pipe; Olivia, big-eyed and grave and wondering; the Longstreets side by side on a couch—Joan hatted and suited and making no effort to hide her haughty displeasure, Kermit spare and tweedy and stiffly erect, his arms folded. Scott Evans fidgeted, a full highball glass in hand; Madge had her knitting.

Why were they all so attentive? Harvey was dead. He hadn't taken his own life. He had died of a heart attack. That was what had happened, and there wasn't any more to know. Oh, the autopsy . . . The Inspector was speaking of it. He said that the time of death fitted the picture, that Harvey appeared to have been dead approximately five days when his body was recovered from the river.

Dace pleated a fold of cloth on a knee. That was right. He had gone over the cliff and down into the river last Friday night. But what difference did it make now? The Inspector was speaking to her. . . . She raised her head.

"Mrs. Allert, did you know, had you any idea, that your husband was suffering from a heart condition?"

Dace said no.

"He never complained of shortness of breath, of pain anywhere?"

She tried to think. "Once in a while he had a rather bad attack of indigestion."

"I see." McKee didn't labor the point, it didn't need elaboration. Men who appeared to be hale and hearty, even men under medical supervision, dropped dead daily under the same circumstances, without the slightest apparent warning.

"What I'd like now," the Scotsman said, "is to go back to Thursday afternoon two weeks ago, the afternoon of the day on which Elfrida Allert had her fatal accident."

Stares, frowns, puzzlement; they told him. Harvey in the house when Dace left it and still there when Olivia arrived at around half past four. Hugh Clavering had come about ten minutes later. He wasn't in the house five minutes.

Clavering said, his brows up, "You're not implying, Inspector, that that scrimmage I had with Harvey did him any lasting damage, that it led to his death up here a week and a half later? I went there to tell him, or rather to tell Dace, about Elfrida and the check and what Elfrida was threatening to do—and he threw a punch at me. I defended myself, that's all."

McKee nodded. "You, Mr. Longstreet? What time did you arrive at the Murray Hill house?"

Kermit stroked his chin meditatively. "I couldn't tell you to the minute. It was long after five. Anyhow, when I got into the house there was no one there—the door was on the latch and I walked in and called."

McKee looked at the statements again. Olivia Wood out posting letters, Clavering out in the street near the iron gates that led to the court waiting for Dace Allert to return; "You didn't see Mr. Longstreet come or go, Mr. Clavering?"

"You could hardly see your hand in front of your face, Inspector. No. The only one I saw was Scott, with a bunch of roses."

Scott Evans reared a belligerent head. His eyes were bloodshot and his hands shaking. He said a little thickly that he hadn't gone into the house at all that day, and took a long swig from his glass. Gerald Straws hadn't arrived at the house until eight o'clock that Thursday night, or so he stated calmly. It remained inconclusive, up in the air.

Seated beside Joan, her head high, her cold eyes inimical, Kermit Longstreet looked mystified. "I'm afraid I don't get the drift of all this, Inspector. . . . What does it matter what happened two weeks ago in New York? Harvey died up here last Friday night. The autopsy findings prove that."

McKee nodded. "The autopsy findings do indeed. The

only trouble is that these findings are false."

He said it quietly, almost casually. It took a minute to penetrate. Surprise, shock, bewilderment, and in someone, knowledge. They were all asking questions except Dace. How *could* the autopsy be wrong? . . . Surely from the condition of the body . . . The doctors ought to know. . . . Within reasonable limits medicine was an exact science. . . . If not, what good was any autopsy?

McKee said that in this case the autopsy had been extremely useful. The contents of the stomach had been analyzed. Some four hours before death Harvey Allert had eaten a meal that consisted of broiled scallops, salad and coffee. He had eaten this meal with a client named Mr. Brubaker in Sweets Restaurant in lower Manhattan at shortly after noon on January the eighth, a day over two weeks ago.

Four hours before death—death on January the eighth . . . Dace was being dragged back to reality. Coming alive was painful. She pushed hair from her forehead, puzzled and in a fog. Her voice was low, it sounded loud in the stillness that gripped the room.

"But Inspector, that can't *be*. . . . Olivia and I saw Harvey alive here, right here in this hall last Friday night, sitting in that chair over there." She raised a hand and pointed to a chair to the left of the fireplace.

McKee shook his head. He said, "No, Mrs. Allert, you didn't see your husband alive. What you saw was your husband's dead body. It had been taken from the place in which it had lain concealed for eight days. That place was in the bottom of the Deep-Freeze in the utility room next to the kitchen in this house."

Complete silence. Not a single sound from any of them. The call from the lab ought to come through soon, McKee thought. . . . Until then—he went on with it. "This is the picture," he said, "this is what happened."

On that distant Thursday afternoon a state trooper had telephoned to the house in the court on Murray Hill with the news that Elfrida Allert had had a bad accident and wasn't expected to live. Harvey had either answered the phone himself, and then had his fatal heart attack, or someone who came in and found him dead took the call. His death prior to Elfrida's would benefit no one, the estate would remain Elfrida's for life and on her death would go to various charities. But on the other hand, McKee said, if Harvey could be shown to be alive *after* Elfrida died, for however short a time, the estate would go to Harvey and through him to his natural heirs. So—Harvey had to be kept alive, or rather it had to be made to look as though he were alive. And this was what had been done.

The first thing was the disposal of the body. The weather was very cold, the temperature stood at five above zero that day. This, McKee emphasized, was one of the chief factors that had made the whole conspiracy to defraud feasible—more than that, it had probably suggested what had actually been done. The Allert car was outside the house in the court and it was growing dark and snowing hard and so there was no danger of being seen. Harvey's body had been carried out to the car, and later on that same night it had been driven up here to this house and placed in the compartment in the Deep-Freeze below the top tray. It was a perfectly safe place. The lower compartment was seldom used. Moreover, Miss Tarbel had gone down to Brideship, the town closest to the hospital, and taken a room in the hotel there so as to be near Elfrida, and the house was empty. Everything Harvey appeared to do thereafter had been done by someone wearing Harvey's outer clothing, his hat and overcoats, and using Harvey's keys and driving his car.

"If you'll stop and think back," McKee said, "you'll recall that no one who knew him ever saw him up close or heard his voice."

Gerald Straws took his dead pipe from between his teeth. "You're wrong there, Inspector. Harvey called Scott Evans."

"Mr. Evans," McKee said, "was not at that time of day, which I believe is usual with him, in a condition to recognize anyone's voice." He ignored Scott's black glance and went on.

The man masquerading as Harvey had driven back to New York that Thursday night in the Benz and had parked it somewhere—men were looking into that angle. On the following night, Friday, the masquerader had entered the house on the court, where he had changed his clothes and recovered Harvey's wallet from the locked desk where his wife had placed it. He was provided with a full set of Harvey's keys, including one for the desk drawer. To avoid running into the arms of a patrolman the masquerader left the house by the rear door. So far so good. Elfrida wasn't expected to live, her death was expected momentarily. Instead she lingered on, so that the pseudo-Harvey had to keep showing up here and there—which was done, very cleverly. Then had come Elfrida's death.

Now, just once more, Harvey had to be shown, established decisively as alive, for the police and everyone else. Hence his appearance in the Hotel Charles in Danbury, where he had supposedly registered as Harold Allen. Up until that point it had all been fair sailing for the masquerader, but there at the Hotel Charles he ran head-on into really heavy weather. In the lobby he bumped into Floss Crosby, who recognized him, and who knew his real identity. McKee said, "One word from the girl and the plot would have blown sky high. Our man lost his head. He asked her up to his room, probably for a drink, and—well you all know what happened."

Dace stirred in her chair. Weight was lifting from her, weight that had been intolerable and that she hadn't known how she was going to bear. Harvey was not a murderer, she had been right. . . . The relief was sweet, healing. It didn't last long. McKee was talking again, about last Friday night here in this house, the night she and Olivia had driven up here through the fog after Madge's call about the finding of the station wagon.

McKee said that there had been no particular danger in the carefully arranged scene set for Dace's benefit that night after she had announced her determination to come up here to the farm. She wouldn't be permitted anywhere near the body. It took clever planning, but everything went off as arranged. She did see her husband sitting relaxed, as she thought, in a chair in front of the fire. Then as she rounded the balcony, the lights went out. If she hadn't obligingly fallen down the stairs she would have received a blow that would have knocked her out, but nothing more than that—she was needed. What better witness than his wife that Harvey Allert was very much alive days after Elfrida's death? Her positive testimony would kill the slightest breath of suspicion, if any such suspicion should ever arise.

The sound McKee had been waiting for came at last, the telephone began to ring. Seated at it Todhunter answered the call, listened, and scribbled on a slip of paper. Hanging up he crossed over and handed the slip of paper to McKee. McKee looked at it and then around at the circle of stiff faces. He said that the man who wore Harvey's clothes, his hat and the two overcoats, first the dark blue vicuña and then the tan tweed ulster, had left an indelible mark on them. Hairs had been collected from the heads of everyone present, sent to the laboratory in New York, and compared with hairs embedded in the hat and the two coats. The man who had masqueraded as Harvey Allert throughout, the man who had killed Floss Crosby in the Hotel Charles in Danbury, was Hugh Clavering—and his partner and helper was Olivia Wood.

More stillness, utter stillness, a moment of it, filled with cold horror. Retreating inside herself but taking it, Dace was distantly aware that after the first slam of shock she wasn't even surprised. She had wandered too long in subterranean caverns filled with the poisonous smoke of fear and surmise. Hugh, the man she had loved, or thought she loved—no wonder the old fire had refused to rekindle itself. Hugh—and Olivia, her big, pretty, rather simple cousin . . . She forced her lids up and looked at Hugh.

His face was closed, shuttered, except for the dark glitter of his eyes. He had seen it coming. He smiled faintly and gave a small shrug. Otherwise he didn't move. The two state troopers were advancing. It was Olivia who moved. Suddenly she was on her feet crying out furiously, hysterically—and futilely. The scrape of a chair, the chair went over, a scream, another . . . "Not me, Inspector. No. No . . . I'm not the one . . ."

Dace threw a hand across her eyes, and tried to close her ears.

"All right now, Dace?"

"I'm splendid, Gerald—simply splendid—need you ask?"

172

Gerald Straws looked pleased at the fierceness in her. But Dace couldn't keep it up, she began to shake again. She and Gerald were alone in the big room. Hugh and Olivia had been taken away, and then the Longstreets and Scott Evans had gone, almost wordlessly. Even Joan Longstreet had been awed into silence, except for that one remark: "Poor Dace, now there'll be nothing for you, not a cent." It wasn't even ill-natured, it was just that money was her first thought, and the Allert money was over the hill. Dace cared nothing about the money—you can't miss what you haven't had. What she did care about was Harvey, that Harvey hadn't killed anyone, that his name had been cleared.

Gerald was standing over her, holding a glass with whiskey in it in his hand. "Here," he said, "drink this," and as she obeyed she thought with a deep shiver of the drink Hugh Clavering had given her out under the trees in the cold darkness late yesterday afternoon. Had Hugh meant to kill her later on?

McKee answered that in a sort of way when he came back into the room. After her outburst Olivia Wood had shut up tight, but Hugh Clavering had talked, a little. Harvey had not only not killed anyone, he hadn't forged any check. Hugh Clavering wasn't in the Murray Hill house on that Thursday two weeks ago by chance. He had gone there with a definite purpose. He had learned the day before, to his shocked surprise, that he was not, as her niece's husband, and Elfrida's close friend, to be the beneficiary of her comfortable personal estate. It was to go to Harvey, every penny of it. It was Hugh who had forged the check on Elfrida's account and sent it to Harvey, knowing Harvey would cash it promptly without asking any questions which wasn't his way.

Clavering's motive was to discredit Harvey in Elfrida's eyes and induce her to do what she really wanted to do, leave her own personal fortune to him instead of to Harvey. McKee said he might have succeeded except for Elfrida's death, which was an accident and nothing but an accident. Clavering had gone to the house that day, with Olivia's knowledge, to put into Harvey's desk the pen with which the forged check had been written. The relationship between Olivia and Hugh was an old affair, it had been

173

going on for years, but neither of them had a cent. Under Hugh's charm and Olivia's large simplicity they were both cool and hard-headed and scheming and ambitious.

"Then why," Dace asked, "if Harvey didn't forge that check, did he want to leave New York in a hurry that day when he came home from the office—why was he so upset?"

McKee said that it must have been because of the money he owed Kermit Longstreet. As far as what had happened up here at the farm late yesterday afternoon, between her and Hugh and what would eventually have happened, McKee said, "Clavering knew Olivia had taken Miss Sturm's bag with the drugs in it and he was afraid of her, of what she might do. You didn't know it but she hated you because you have everything she wanted. In my opinion you would have been permitted to live for a while as Harvey's heir—Miss Wood is your cousin and would inherit from you, when the proper time came to act—which it would have. However, if later on you'd married Hugh Clavering—after that—well, I don't know. It might have come to a tug of war between the two of them. In that case it's impossible to say."

Gerald Straws cleared his throat. "Inspector, did Harvey take the call about Elfrida from the state trooper that Thursday in the Murray Hill house?"

"No," McKee said, "according to Clavering, this is what happened. When Olivia Wood admitted Clavering she had just found Harvey dead on the living-room floor. They were standing there looking down at him appalled when the phone rang. Clavering took the call—and that was when the whole scheme began.

"The rest you're familiar with. The maid Gertrude came upstairs and found Clavering in the hall and he pretended to let himself out. When the maid was gone he and Olivia Wood got Harvey's body into the Benz, in the snow-filled court where the garage attendant had parked it earlier. Then Olivia drove the car off and waited in it while Clavering intercepted you, Mrs. Allert, and planted the forgery charge against Harvey firmly in your mind."

"And that call to the Hotel Charles in Danbury to have Harvey paged—wasn't that a—a mistake?" Gerald asked.

McKee said, "Olivia Wood made the call in order to

identify Harvey as Harold Allen, Harvey using a false name and on the run, to prepare for his death later." It was a mistake as things turned out, but after the unanticipated murder of Floss Crosby and his fast getaway from the Charles, Clavering had no opportunity to get in touch with Olivia Wood in time to stop her call. His chief objective was to put the station wagon out of sight, which he did, in the old barn near the south gate and get into his own car parked there in readiness to resume his supposed search for Harvey. Actually, McKee remarked, it was Elfrida's protracted death which had driven them to these twists and turns, but they were both clever people and they were equal to it—the stakes were high.

Dace sat silent looking ahead of her while McKee and Gerald talked. Dreary, dreary day, but with gleams of comfort in it, like the colorless winter sunlight falling palely through the windows. Harvey was not anything they said he had been. . . . They were waiting for Madge Tarbel, who was going to drive back to New York with them and stay with Dace for a while, and Dace wished Madge would hurry—she had a passionate longing to get away, to get out of the house, clear of it. . . . But it would only be a few minutes now. . . . Presently McKee went out of the room in answer to a summons from a trooper. Gerald remained where he was, leaning against the fireplace loading a pipe.

Sore and beaten, Dace looked up and said out of a pause, "You knew about Hugh and Olivia, didn't you, Gerald?"

He struck a match. "I suspected it," he said. "Little things . . . I don't know—but anyhow I did suspect them. I was watching Olivia's apartment to see whether Clavering was going to turn up there when you caught me out the other day."

"Why didn't you tell me?"

Gerald tossed a second match into the fire. "I had no proof—and you wouldn't have believed me without it. . . . Besides—I didn't want to hurt you."

Dace looked at him skeptically. How often Gerald, with whom from the first she had had a feeling of affinity, of being on the same plain and oddly at home, how often he

175

had subtly rebuffed her when she would have made friends with him, from the very beginning. She said, "You never liked me, Gerald, and you know it."

He nodded. "Right." His pipe still wasn't lit. He struck another match and looked at her over the flame. "No, Dace, I never liked you. I loved you from the first moment I saw you, set eyes on you. That was the trouble. . . ."

He stopped speaking as the door opened and Madge stuck her head in. "Ready, folks? If you are, I am."

Dace was ready for nothing. She had just had a terrific shock. Gerald . . . It seemed impossible to believe. She didn't answer, and Gerald didn't seem to expect an answer. She got shakily to her feet. But somehow the sunlight coming more widely through the windows was suddenly brighter and the air easier to breathe as Gerald helped her into her coat and they left the room and the house with his steadying hand on her arm.